Zucker & Levett & Loeb co.

Practical Plating and Polishing

Zucker & Levett & Loeb co.

Practical Plating and Polishing

ISBN/EAN: 9783337292621

Printed in Europe, USA, Canada, Australia, Japan

Cover: Foto ©Andreas Hilbeck / pixelio.de

More available books at **www.hansebooks.com**

...TICAL

P... ...D POLISHING,

WITH

...ickel-Plating and Polishing

...cycle Work....

GIVING

TH... ...ST APPROVED METHODS

OF

...ng all Metals for

...Polishing.

ILLUS...

PUBLISHED B...

ZUCKER & LEVETT & LOEB CO.,

NEW YORK.

PREFACE.

In compiling this work we have endeavored to make it practical in every detail, wording it in concise and simple language, and avoiding technical terms as much as possible. We trust it will prove of benefit to our patrons and platers in general.

NEW YORK, April, 1897.

CONTENTS.

INTRODUCTORY.

The sources of current used for electro-plating are Dynamo Electric Machines and Batteries.

Until the introduction of plating dynamos, about 50 years ago, electro-plating was done exclusively by batteries of various kinds, but at the present time the dynamo has almost entirely superseded them, except for amateur work and where power is not available. The reasons for this are many. In the first place, though the first outlay is more for a dynamo, it is far more economical in the end, as the exciting fluids of batteries have to be changed very frequently and they need constant attention ; whereas a dynamo, with the ordinary care that would be bestowed on any piece of machinery, will last for years. In the second place, the current obtained from a dynamo can always be depended upon to be constant, which is very essential in plating, whereas with a battery there are incessant changes going on, which makes the current very irregular. Another objection to batteries is that they give off fumes which are injurious to the health. This latter objection can be overcome however by placing the batteries in a closet especially built for same, with a wooden shute leading from the top into the chimney flue to carry off the fumes.

CHAPTER I.

DYNAMO ELECTRIC MACHINES.

Electro-Deposition by Dynamo. As the Dynamo Electric Machine is at the present day the best and most economical source of current for electro-plating (and as this is a practical book on electro-plating and not a history of that art) we deem it proper that it should receive our first attention.

It is not our intention to trace, step by step, the evolution of the plating dynamo, nor to note the changes and improvements that have been made from the time of Faraday's discovery up to the present day, but we will describe, as clearly and briefly as possible, the electro-plating dynamo, as it appears to-day, using our Improved American Giant Dynamo as an example. (See Figs. 1 and 2.) Those who are desirous of knowing the numerous improvements that have been made since the introduction of the first plating dynamo, we refer to the numerous text books on this subject.

A dynamo electric machine consists of the following principal parts :

1. The revolving portion, called the armature, in which the electro motive force is developed which produces the current

2. The field magnets, between which the armature revolves.

3. The commutator, by which the currents developed in the armature are caused to flow in the same direction.

4. The brushes that rest on the commutator, which are used to collect and transmit the current generated in the armature.

5.   The brackets, which support the armature.

6.   The base, to which the brackets and field castings are bolted.

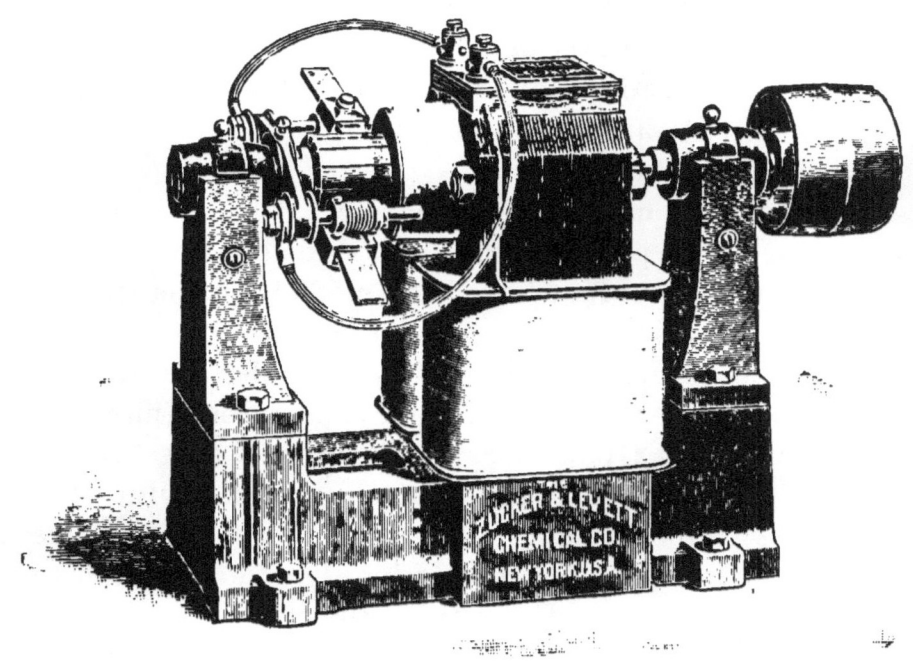

Fig. 1.   Improved American Giant Dynamo.   Types 2 and 3.

We have spared no trouble nor expense in designing and building our Improved American Giant Dynamos, and we feel confident that we have reached a state approaching nearer to perfection than has ever been attained before.   Whenever there are any improvements discovered we do not hesitate to apply them, no matter what they may cost, as we believe the only way to retain the prestige we have acquired is by keeping thoroughly up with the times.

The machines are of the inverted horse-shoe type, having a laminated field, made of the best Swedish iron in the smaller and a special cast iron, equal to wrought iron, in the larger sizes.

The armature is thoroughly laminated to prevent all possible heating due to "Foucault" or eddy currents, and the armature heads are covered to prevent any dirt or oil from entering same, also to prevent the wire from receiving mechanical injury.

The commutator bars are drop-forged copper and are thoroughly insulated with mica throughout.

The machines are shunt wound. and so proportioned that it is impossible for them to reverse, that is, the current to flow through the solution in the opposite direction to what it should, an evil so often encountered and dreaded by the plater.

The bearings are made of a special alloy, harder than phosphor bronze, and are provided with an automatic oiling device, which keeps the shaft of the armature constantly lubricated.

The Improved American Giant Dynamos are unexcelled in point of simplicity. All the parts are in sight and easily accessible, and the armature can be removed and replaced by any one in a few minutes.

We furnish with each dynamo a diagram and full directions how to keep the same in proper order, also how to remove the armature and other parts.

As a dynamo plays a very important part in the Art of electro-plating, great care should be exercised in selecting one, and the following points should be observed :

1. The workmanship and material should be of the best, and all parts should be of ample size, especially the commutator and bearings. The bearings should have

self-oiling attachments, thereby insuring thorough lubrication.

2. The machine should run without sparking at the commutator, as sparking causes the commutator to wear away rapidly and unevenly, so that it has to be frequently taken out and turned down.

3. The brushes and holders should be of simple design so that they may be easily kept clean, and should have a simple and efficient tension device so that the proper pressure may be obtained at all times.

4. A dynamo should be able to keep up its voltage or pressure under a full load, as the steadiness of the current depends on this.

5. In purchasing a dynamo it is always well to select one of a little larger capacity than is actually needed, as the wear and tear on a dynamo, like on an engine or boiler, is much less when not run to its fullest capacity.

CHAPTER II.

ELECTRICAL TERMS.

We will have occasion in the following pages to use a few electrical terms, and for those who are not already acquainted with same we give the following information:

Volt.—A volt is the unit of electrical pressure, and is used the same as pound pressure is used when applied to a steam boiler or water pipe.

Ampere.—An ampere is the unit of quantity, and is used to denote amount of current flowing, in the same way that gallons or cubic feet per minute are used when applied to steam or water.

Ohm or Resistance.—An ohm is the unit of resistance, and corresponds to the friction that exists where water is flowing through a pipe. For example: To use the water pipe as an illustration, suppose that at 100 lb. pressure, at the reservoir or pump, a pipe of given dimensions delivers one hundred gallons of water per minute. If we increase the pressure from one hundred to two hundred pounds the delivery would be increased from one hundred to two hundred gallons. Now suppose that with the original pressure of 100 lbs. the length of the pipe be doubled (or the area reduced to ½) only one-half the amount of water, or 50 gallons, would be delivered.

The above examples may be applied to electricity by using a wire in place of a pipe and volts and amperes instead of pressure and quantity.

Therefore it can be readily seen that there exists a definite relation between the above electrical terms, namely; volt, ampere and ohm.

CHAPTER III.

DIRECTIONS FOR SETTING UP AND OPERATING THE IMPROVED AMERICAN GIANT DYNAMO.

Position.—Select a convenient dry position for the machine, where there is plenty of light, if possible. Set on a suitable base, so that there will be no shaking or vibration. Do not have the machine near any polishing machinery, as the emery and dust will soon ruin the best dynamo.

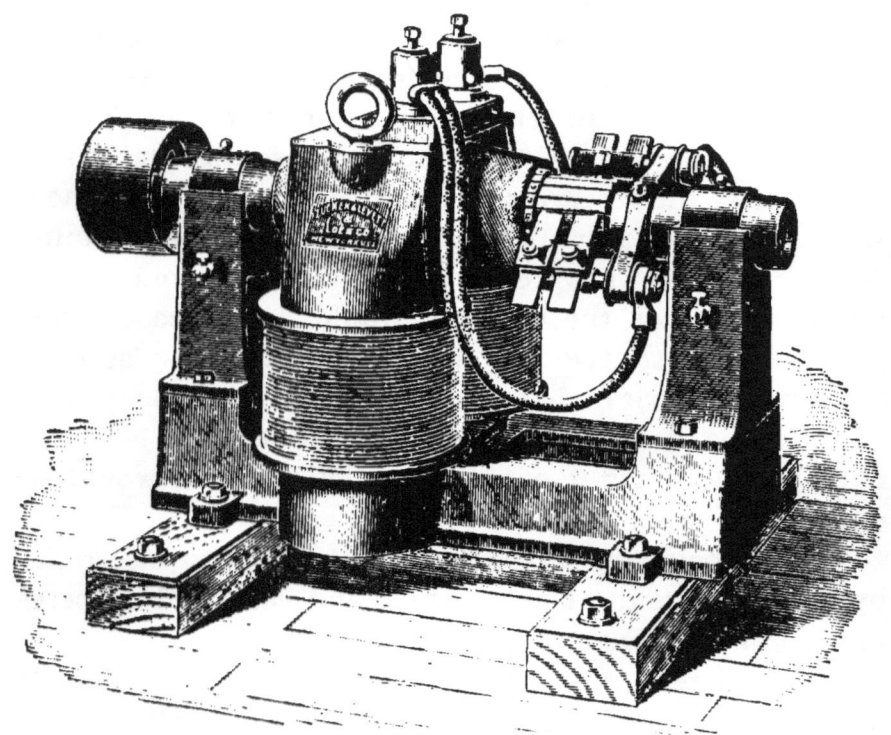

Fig. 2. Improved American Giant Dynamo. Types 4 to 8.

Belting.—Use a good quality pliable belt of the full width of the pulley. Make the lacing as smooth as possible. A great deal of unnecessary trouble is caused by patching up old scrap belts to use on dynamos. The tension of the belt should be just sufficient to prevent it slipping on full load. If any tighter it only wears out the bearings. If possible the dynamo should be placed so as to have a slanting rather than a vertical belt, and so that the under side of the belt does the pulling.

Speed.—Run the machine the exact speed that is stamped on the name plate. If the dynamo does not do its work, find out whether the trouble is not due to the speed being too low. In case the dynamo does not run fast enough do not change its pulley. To increase the speed, change the pulley on countershaft. If necessary, a larger pulley may be put on dynamo to reduce the speed to that marked on the plate.

Oil.—Use only a good, light quality of mineral oil. Never use animal or vegetable oils. They may be more expensive, but are not as good, and are liable to gum and corrode the bearings. While the machine is running pour oil into the oil boxes slowly until lubricating ring is seen to work well. If too full the oil will drip out of the ends of the boxes. If too little is put in, the oil ring will fly around and throw the oil. When the oil is dirty draw it out through the drip cocks and refill

Care and Cleanliness.—Keep the machine clean, especially the brushes and commutator. Never use a file on the commutator, but clean off same once or twice a day with a clean rag, and if necessary with very fine sand paper, say No. o. Then put the smallest possible amount of oil on the end of the finger and rub over the commutator. Never put enough oil on so that the commutator looks greasy and dirty. *Never use Emery*, as it will cut the commutator and the brushes badly; this is important. If strip copper brushes are used they should be filed to a proper bevel, when necessary, in a jig provided for that purpose. Wire Gauze Brushes cannot be easily filed but can be trimmed with scissors, which

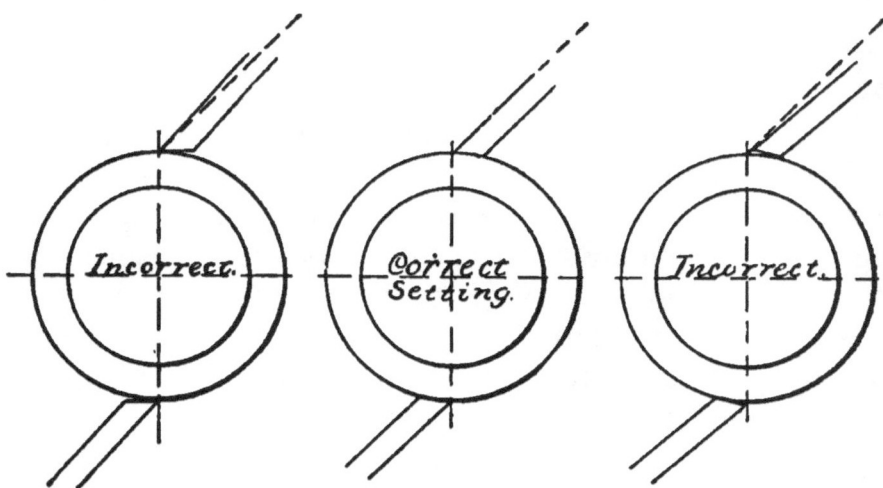

Fig. 3. Position of Brushes on Commutator.

must be carefully done. As the wire brushes are of a soft and spongy nature, it is essential, to insure good running, that they be handled carefully while being inserted and adjusted, so that they may retain their shape.

Tension and Position of Brushes.—The brushes should be adjusted to make a light but positive contact. They should be given a fair and even bedding on the commutator. If they are badly adjusted and bear on the heel or toe, or on one side, the machine is liable to spark. See Fig. 3.

A broad, not a heavy contact is required. The brushes and rocker arm are set correctly on leaving the factory, but it will not do to trust to their being correct when the machine is received, as the rocker arm may have become shifted in transit. Loosen the clamp screw and move the brushes forward or backward while the dynamo is generating until a place is found where it runs without sparking. Never try to regulate the current by changing the position of the rocker arm. The regulation should be made by means of switchboards, or resistance boards, which we can provide for the purpose.

Plug Switch.—Some of our dynamos have a triple plug switch on the terminal board, as shown in Fig. 4, the object of which is to increase or decrease the intensity

Fig. 4. Plug Switch.

of the current. When a small amount of work is in the tanks, the dynamo should be run without any of the plugs *AAA* being inserted in the metal plate *B*, and as more work is put into the tanks, the plugs may be inserted one by one in order to keep the voltage constant. It does not matter which hole is used first. The cut shows one of the plugs inserted in the metal plate. There are three holes in the wood to hold the plugs when not in

18

use. Do not hammer the plugs in but twist them in lightly with the fingers. It is frequently unnecessary to use these plugs on certain kinds of work even with a full load, as the dynamo will give sufficient intensity without them. It is better to cut down the intensity of the current by the withdrawal of the plugs than by putting a resistance into the circuit by means of switchboards, though both are necessary at times.

Fig. 5 shows two views of the Multipolar American Giant Dynamo, which is a six pole steel machine with a commutator at each end of the armature. This style dynamo is built of such generous proportions that it can be run at the low speed of 400 to 500 revolutions per minute with very little friction and comparatively no heat.

Heretofore one of the weak points of very large plating dynamos was an insufficient brush surface. This fault has been overcome in the 1896 type of the Improved American Giant Dynamos, they having double the brush surface per ampere of any low voltage machine built.

As low voltage dynamos require very large commutators, the arrangement of two commutators was adopted with the view of giving ample surface for collecting the current. The two windings of the armature connecting with each commutator are carefully insulated from each other, and in case of an accident to one of the windings, the machine could be run on something like a two-thirds load on the remaining winding until repairs could be effected.

When requested, these dynamos are connected with the windings either in parallel or in series. As ordinarily used the windings are connected in parallel, but in the case of a plating room where solutions requiring

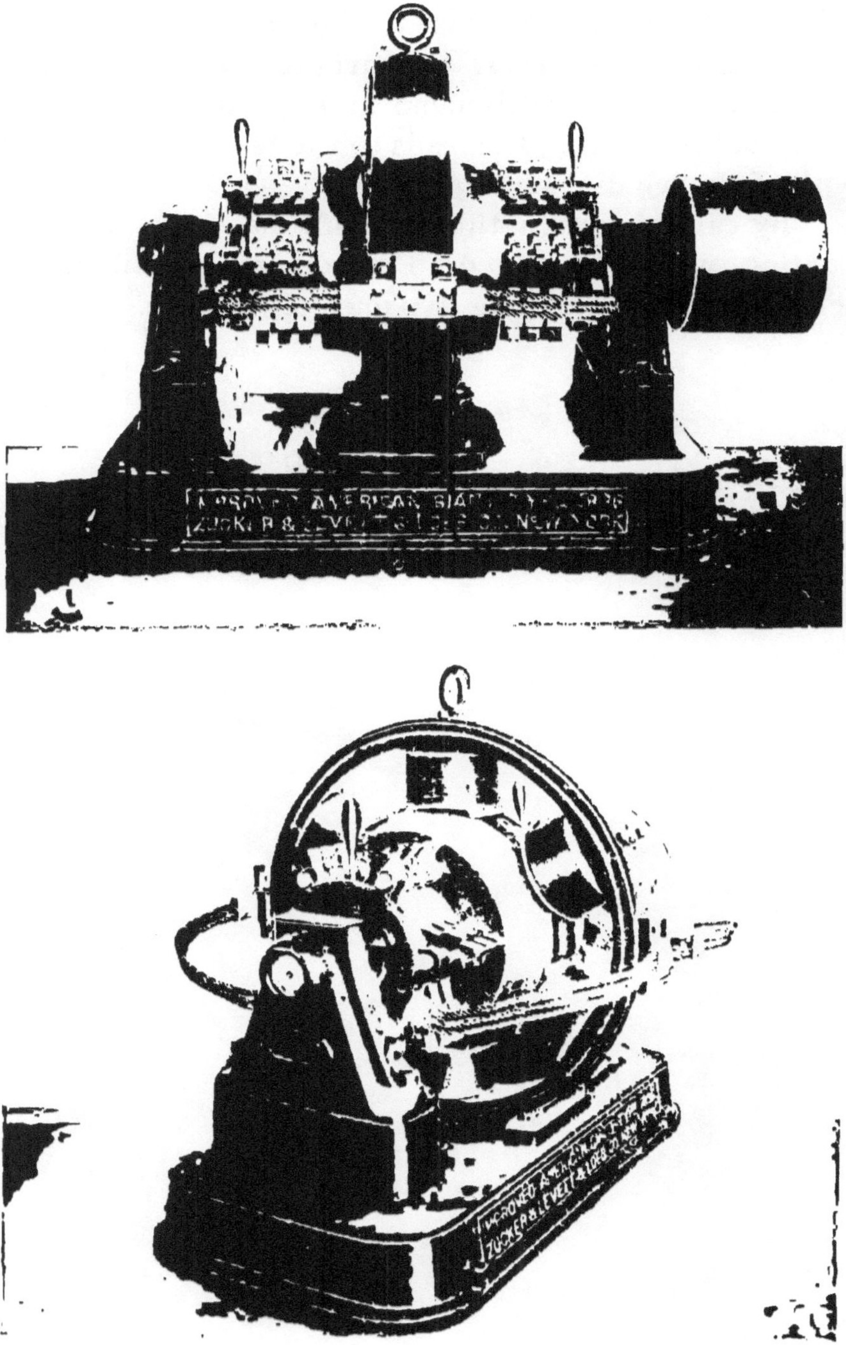

Fig 5. Two Views of the Multipolar American Giant Dynamos.

different intensities are used, the windings may be connected in series, as by this arrangement the current can be taken from the dynamo at two different voltages by simply connecting the leads to the terminals of one or both of the windings.

By careful design this machine has been built self exciting, with almost no drop in voltage, a result never before obtained in plating dynamos of this size.

CHAPTER IV.

ELECTRICAL ARRANGEMENT OF A PLATING PLANT.

The connections between the dynamo, switchboards and tanks, should be of the best in order to secure good results. Also, the location of the dynamo has an important bearing on the cost in large plating rooms.

We shall consider this subject under three heads :

1. Arrangement of Dynamo and Tanks.
2. Size of conductors.
3. Joints, or connections.

Arrangement of Dynamo and Tanks.—The dynamo and tanks should be placed as near together as possible. If two or three tanks only are used a suitable arrangement is to have the tanks in one line with the dynamo at one end of the line. See Fig. 6.

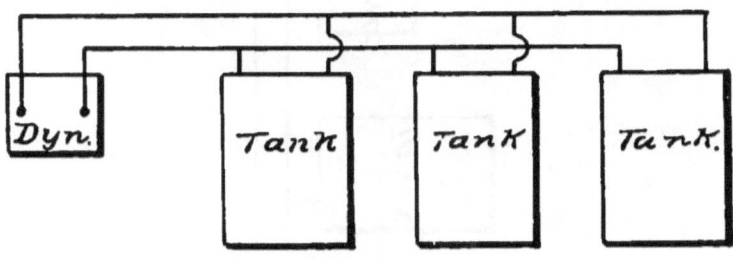

Figure 6.

If a large number of tanks is used and it is desirable on account of convenience to have them in one line, it would be well to have the dynamo in the center of the line, (as shown in Fig. 7), as the main conductors would only have to be one-half the diameter (which would be ¼ the weight) that would be required if the dynamo was at one end of the line, thereby saving about $\frac{3}{4}$ of the weight of copper.

If on the other hand, an extra large number of tanks is used it would be considerably more economical to

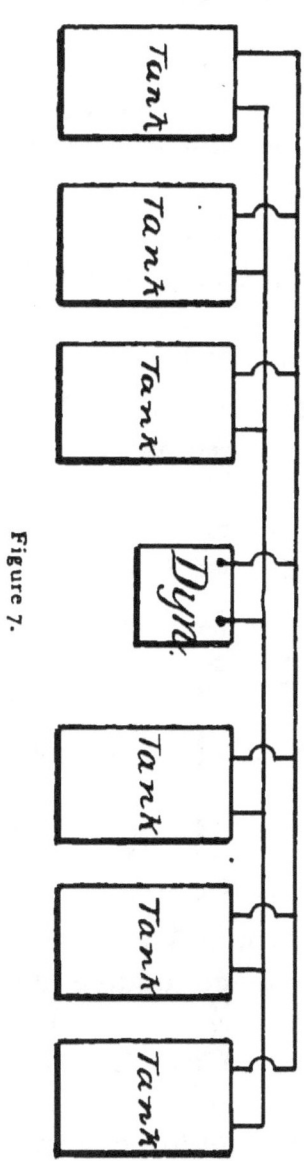

Figure 7.

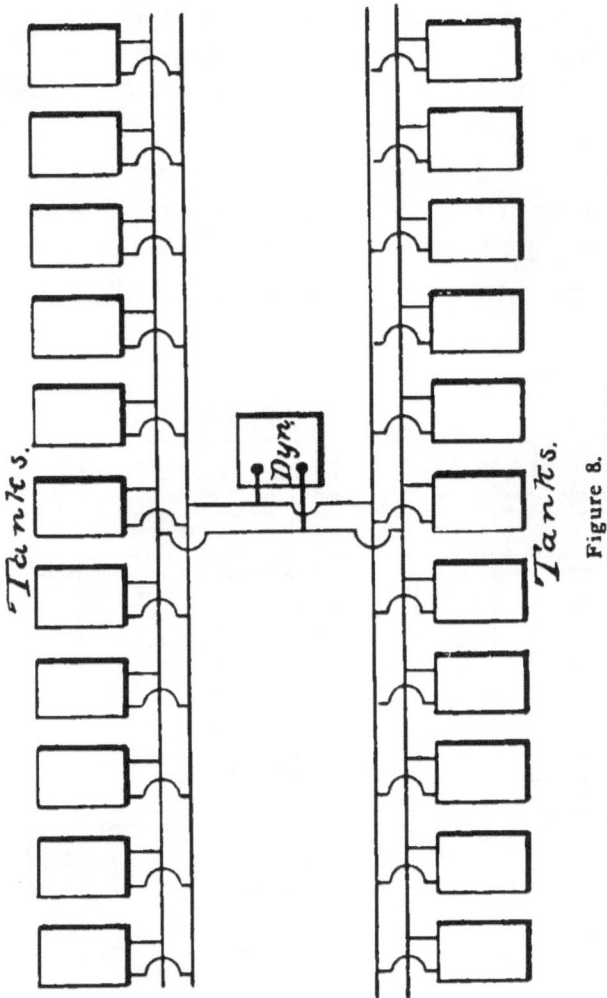

Figure 8.

arrange them in two parallel lines, comparatively near
together, with the dynamo between the lines and an
equal distance from the ends, (see Fig. 8), effecting a
still further saving in the copper over the second
arrangement. The advantage of proper arrangement
of tanks increases rapidly with the size of the plant,
the saving in large plants amounting in some cases
to several hundreds of dollars.

The reason for this will be shown later on, under
the heading of "The Size of Conductors." In the
above arrangements it is immaterial what kind or how
many kinds of solution are used.

In many large plating plants running only one kind
of solution requiring a low voltage or pressure, such as
acid copper, nickel or silver, the following system is the
best, as it maintains exactly the same voltage or pressure

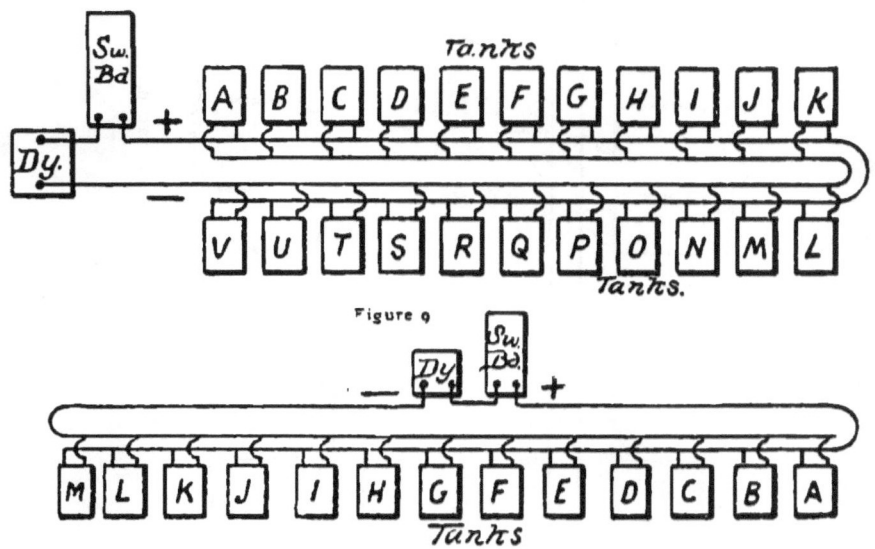

Figure 9.

Figure 10.

at each tank. This will enable the plater to control all
the tanks with one switchboard, and economically insures
an even deposition of metal, which could only be obtained in other systems of wiring by the expenditure of
a large amount of money in copper conductors.

In the common system of wiring, the tank farthest
from the dynamo has the least pressure, on account of

the resistance of the main conductors, though by making these excessively large the difference would be reduced to a minimum, but at the expense of a great outlay.

An examination of Figures 9 and 10 of the system under consideration, reveals the fact that each tank is electrically the same distance away from the dynamo, and therefore they will all have the same voltage, though that voltage or pressure would be determined by the size of the main conductors.

For example, if we start from tank A we see that as we go toward tanks B, C, D, etc., while we are getting farther away from the dynamo on the + or positive conductor we are getting exactly the same distance nearer to the dynamo on the — or negative conductor. Therefore as we go from tank to tank the increasing resistance on the positive conductor is compensated for by the decreasing resistance on the negative conductor.

Though the conditions in different plating plants vary greatly, the systems and arrangements given above will be found to cover all ordinary contingencies. In particular cases where more exact information is required we will be pleased to submit a plan and specifications showing the most economical and practical system of wiring, etc., provided we are given a plan of the room and informed of the number, size and location of tanks and the kinds of solution and work to be run.

The Size of Conductors.—As has been stated before, the tanks should be as near as possible to the dynamo, or considerable electrical power will be lost in the conductors, unless the size of same is increased. This increase is as the square of the distance. For example, if a dynamo carried a certain load satisfactorily, using a half inch conductor, the distance from the tanks being

·30 feet, if the distance is increased to 60 feet the size conductors necessary would have to be increased to about $\frac{3}{4}''$ diameter or four times the weight ; if increased to 120 feet it would be necessary to use $1''$ conductors, which would increase the weight of copper 16 times over the original weight of the 30 foot conductors. So it can be readily seen that unless great care is used in laying out a plating plant, the conductors will increase the cost of same to a considerable extent.

The holes in the binding posts of our dynamos are made to hold the proper size connecting wires or main conductors so that the farthest tank may be 40 feet away from the dynamo. If any of the tanks are farther away the diameter of the main conductors should be increased as above stated Outside of the matter· of cost the connecting wires and main conductors can never be too large, as the larger they are the less power will be lost.

The size of the connecting wire between the main conductors and tanks depends upon the number of tanks. If only 1 tank, of course the full size of the main conductors should be run to it; if 2 tanks the diameter of connecting wires to each tank should be about $\frac{2}{3}$ that of the main conductors ; if 3 to 7 tanks, about $\frac{1}{2}$ the diameter ; if 8 to 15, about $\frac{1}{3}$ the diameter ; if 16 to 25, about $\frac{1}{4}$ the diameter. ·

As for the tank rods, no particular attention need be paid to them from an electrical standpoint, as the mechanical strength required always makes them large enough to give ample conductivity. If more definite instructions are required we will be pleased to submit plans and specifications as to the most economical mode of wiring, etc., as stated before.

Joints or Connections.—Since the currents used in plating are of large amperage and generally of extremely low voltage it is evident that they must have a path to travel on from the dynamo through the tank or tanks and back through the switchboards (if switchboards are used) to the dynamo, of very low resistance ; otherwise a large proportion of the pressure will be lost.

The first joint that is made is the connection between the dynamo and the main wires or rods. The holes in the dynamo binding posts should be carefully cleaned with sandpaper or a scraper. The ends of the wires or rods should be of a diameter to just fit the holes in the binding posts.

Wires smaller than the holes in binding posts should never be used. This is contrary to ordinary practice and many platers will disregard the manufacturers' advice and put in wires of one-half or even one-quarter the size recommended and required.

Where the main conductors are small, say from about ¼″ to ½″, they are often started from the dynamo and run their whole length in one piece without break.

Where larger sizes are used, from about ¾″ and upward, the copper comes in lengths of about 12 feet. The common way of connecting these rods is to place the ends together and connect them by a casting or coupling, each rod being held by one or two small set screws. This construction is extremely bad and may be compared to connecting two gas pipes by putting the ends together and wrapping the joint with a few layers of muslin. Some of the gas would propably go through the pipe, but no one could tell how much. It would be safe, however, to predict a big leakage from the joints.

In big rods carrying heavy currents the joints should be as carefully made as in gas or steam pipe. The best way is to use brass pipe fittings. Both the fittings and the ends of the rods should be tinned, and after being screwed solidly together should be sweated.

If, however, the above is not practicable and it is necessary to use couplings, take precautions to have the rods fit snugly the whole length of the couplings. In one of the best equipped plating rooms in the country all joints in the main conductors are made with T couplings tapped for the 1¼″ main conductor and a ½″ branch to each tank. The rods are cut to just the right length, so that a joint comes over each tank. There is practically an even voltage all over the whole room, which is a large one, about 50x100 feet. Moreover, each tank is supplied with a plug cut-out, (see Fig. 11)' which

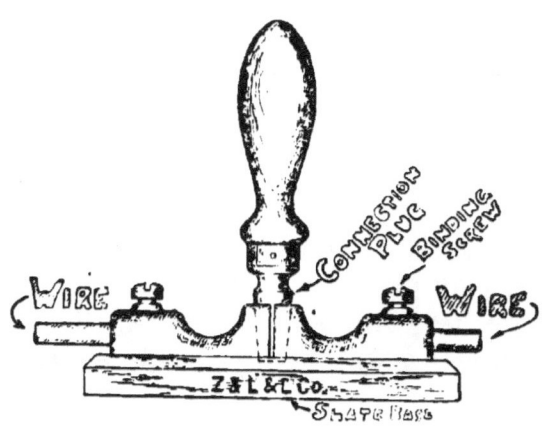

Fig 11.   Plug Cut-out

enables the operator to cut out any one of the tanks at will, without interfering with the other tanks.

Connections may be made between round rods and wires, as illustrated in Fig. 12.

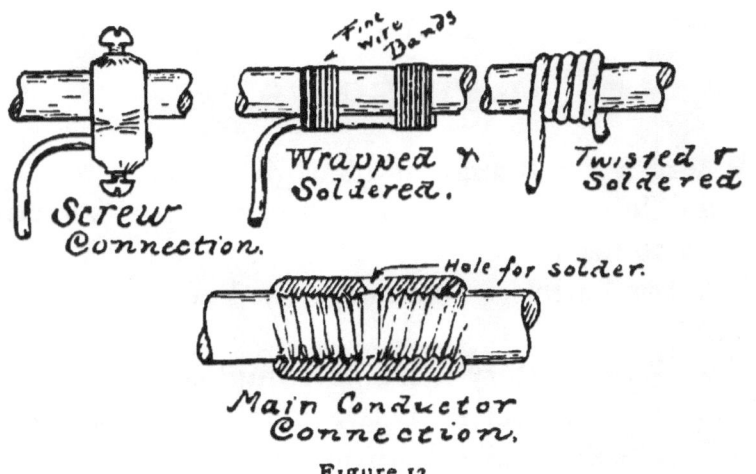

Screw Connection.

Wrapped r Soldered.

Twisted r Soldered

Fine wire Bands

Hole for solder.

Main Conductor Connection.

Figure 12.

It is not by any means essential to use round rods for conductors, as any other shape is just as good electrically, and some are more convenient to handle. They must, however, be of the same weight per foot as the proper size round rod.

CHAPTER V.

BATTERIES.

Where a small amount of work is to be done, or it is impossible to get power for a dynamo, it is sometimes necessary to use batteries for plating.

The two batteries commonly used are the Smee and Bunsen.

The Smee battery is a single fluid cell and consists of a pair of zinc plates between which is a plate of carbon. The fluid is sulphuric acid, diluted about one part acid to seven or eight parts water.

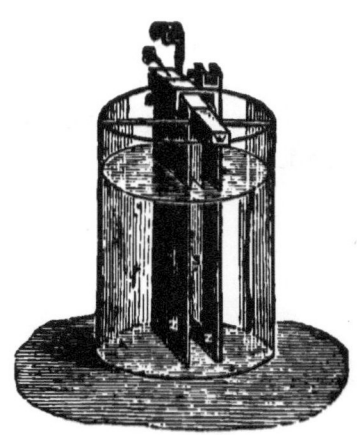

Figure 13. Smee Battery.

The principal objections to the Smee battery are :

1. Plating requires from ¾ to 1½ volts for silver to 4 to 8 volts for brass. The Smee battery gives from .5 to .6 volts. Therefore it is necessary to use, even for the smallest amount of work, about 2 to 4 cells for silver and 7 to 12 cells for brass.

2. The Smee battery when giving its full current

does not utilize the full force obtainable from the consumption of zinc in acid owing to the fact that hydrogen gas is generated in quantity and deposited on the negative plate. This introduces a high internal resistance and cuts down the current sometimes over one-half. As the quantity of hydrogen on the plates is very variable it follows that the current is also uncertain.

The Bunsen Battery.—This cell consists of a porous cup, either round or oblong, placed inside of a glass or earthenware jar, of similar shape. The zinc plate is rolled into a cylindrical form and placed outside of the porous cup. The carbon plate, or plates, are placed inside the porous cup, which is filled nearly full of commercial nitric acid of 30 degrees Beaume. The solution in the outer jar is dilute sulphuric acid of : 1 part acid to 7 parts water or 1 part acid to 17 parts water.

Figure 14.

With the Bunsen Battery we get about 1.7 volts per cell or three times that of the old Smee cell. The introduction of the porous cup and use of two acids effectually prevents the deposition of gas on the negative plate, making this battery very powerful and even in its action and economical in its operation. This battery has a very large zinc surface resulting in large quantity of current and a low resistance, which means small internal waste.

In both batteries the zincs should be thoroughly amalgamated with mercury. This is done by dipping the plates in dilute sulphuric acid and immersing in mercury; or by pouring the mercury on them and working it over the entire surface with a cloth or coarse brush.

In using the Bunsen battery care should be taken not to spill any of the nitric acid into the sulphuric acid solution.

To obtain the required voltage or pressure the cells are connected in series, that is, the carbon of one cell is joined to the zinc of the next, and so on throughout the line; the carbon on one end of the series is joined to the anodes, the zinc on the other end to the work.

By this arrangement we get the force of each cell added to that of the next. Assuming for any given work that it is necessary to have $4\frac{1}{2}$ volts and that each cell gives $1\frac{1}{2}$ volts, it would be necessary to put three cells in series.

We beg to repeat what we have said regarding batteries, that we do not advocate the use of same in any case except when a party has no power or has very little work to be done, as batteries are expensive and uncleanly. We should not recommend them in any case where the amount of solution exceeds 25 gallons.

There are three arrangements for connecting batteries: Series, Parallel and Series-Parallel.

We give a sketch on the opposite page of these

33

Series arrangement.

P N

Parallel arrangement

N P

Series - Parallel arrangement.

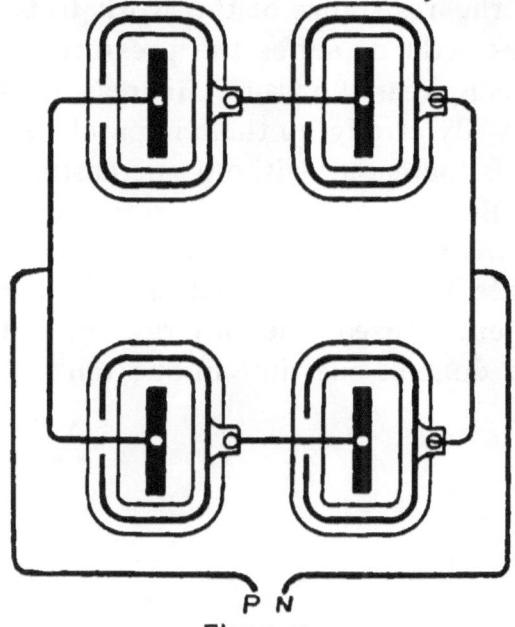

P N

Figure 15.

different modes of connection. In the Series arrangement it will be seen that the negative pole or zinc is connected with the positive pole or carbon of the next cell, the zinc being connected with the following carbon of the next cell, and so on. In the Parallel arrangement the carbons are all connected together and the zincs are all connected together. In the Series-Parallel arrangement the carbon of the first cell is connected with the carbon of the third cell, the zinc of the first cell is connected with the carbon of the second cell, the zinc of the second cell is connected with the zinc of the fourth cell, and the zinc of the third cell with the carbon of the fourth. By referring to the figure on the preceding page this can be traced out so that the inexperienced can determine.

Now we will see when it is advisable to use these different arrangements. To determine the number of cells to be used in series one must be guided by the amount and the resistance of the work to be done. By arranging the cells in series the pressure or voltage of the current is increased without increasing the quantity or amperage. By arranging them in parallels the quantity or amperage is increased without increasing the pressure or voltage. By arranging them in series parallel both the pressure and quantity is increased. Arrangement in parallel is little if ever used in plating. The Series-Parallel arrangement is used when a large amount of work is desired to be done at one time in one tank.

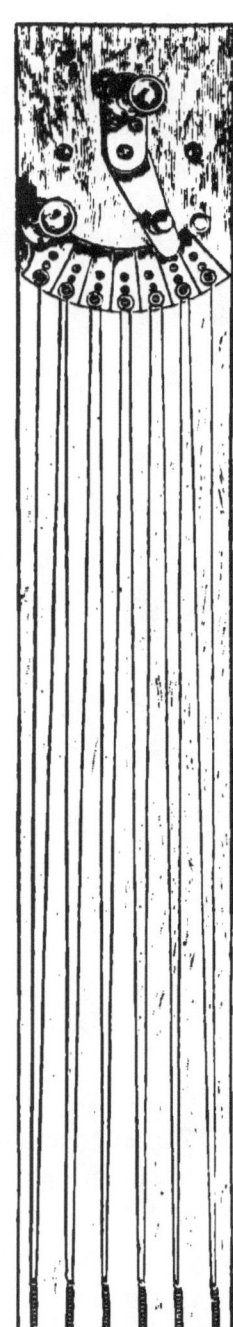

Figure 16.

CHAPTER VI.

SWITCHBOARDS AND VOLTMETERS.

Switchboards or resistance boards are used to regulate the current. The longer and finer the various wires on a switchboard, the greater the resistance and the smaller the current.

It is thus possible, by using a switchboard having a number of wires of various sizes, to so regulate the current that any required amount may be allowed to flow through the tank or tanks in series with same.

As the quality and also the weight of the deposit depends upon the current density, (or number of amperes per square foot), it is necessary as a rule to use switchboards in circuit with the tanks. Where only one tank of several kinds of solution is used, it is necessary to have a switchboard for each tank. Where, however, several tanks of the same kind of solution are used, it is much handier to regulate them all from one switchboard.

For example, in the plating rooms of large bicycle factories, it is customary to run only one or two tanks of copper solution and several of nickel solution. In this case the nickel tanks can all be con trolled from one large switchboard and the copper tanks can be connected to the main conductors between the dynamo and switchboard, so as to get the whole pressure of the current.

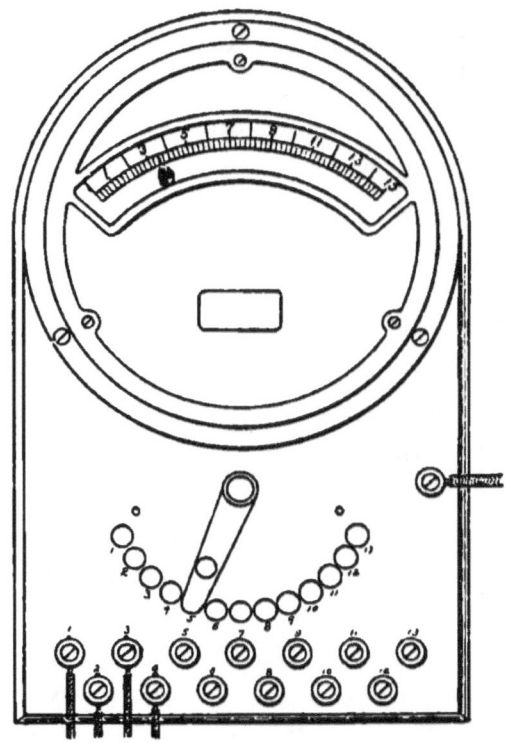

Figure 17.

Voltmeter.—A voltmeter' is used to show the pressure or voltage. The cut above (figure 17) represents a special voltmeter which can be connected with any number of solution tanks, and by means of which the plater can determine the voltage entering any of the same by simply moving the lever to the corresponding button.

With one of these special voltmeters to indicate the strength of the current, and a switchboard or switchboards

37

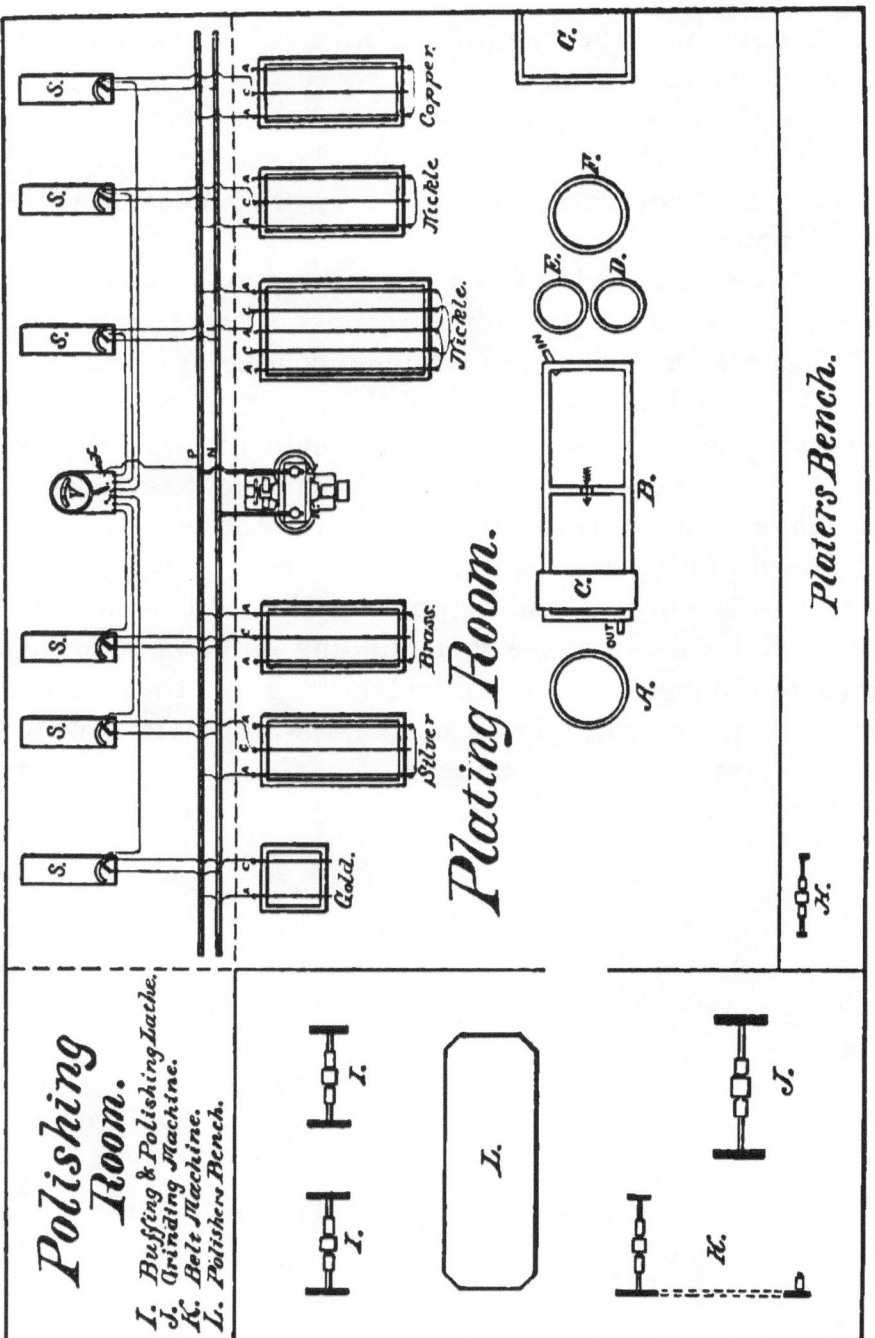

Figure 18.

to regulate same, the operator will always have the current under absolute control.

On the preceding page is shown a diagram of a complete plating room, showing a switchboard for each tank and a special voltmeter, and how they are connected with the dynamo and tanks.

The dynamo being fixed as per directions on pages 14 to 20, connect the positive binding post of same, by means of a heavy wire or cable, to the main conductor P or anode rod running along the wall, and the negative to the main conductor N. Connect the main conductor P with the anode rod of tank A. If more than one anode rod is used in a tank, connect them together at the other end of tank, as shown in diagram. From cathode rod of tank C, run a wire to one of the binding posts of the switchboard, S. Run a fine wire from the same binding post to one of the lower binding posts of the voltmeter, V. From the binding post, X, on the right hand side of the voltmeter, run a fine wire to the main conductor, P. Connect the other binding post of switchboard, S, to the main conductor, N.

CHAPTER VII.

TANKS.

Tanks which are used to hold electro plating solution should be made of well seasoned two inch pine heavily bolted and dovetailed together, and made in such a manner that they are absolutely free from leakage. They should be lined with material that is not acted upon by the solution which is to be placed in the tank.

When not in use, all wooden tanks should be filled with water, for no matter how well a tank is made or how good the material, it will in time dry out and crack if left empty.

For nickel plating, a tank should be lined with a mixture of asphaltum and pitch.

For copper, brass, silver, gold, or any plating solution containing cyanide, it is better to line the tank with paraffine, which should be well ironed into the wood.

Enameled lined iron tanks are best for all hot cyanide solutions, although many use plain iron tanks for hot cyanide of copper solution.

When iron tanks are used great care is requisite in order to prevent the copper rods or tubes used for suspending the anodes and work in the bath from coming in contact with the tank, which would cause a short circuit.

CHAPTER VIII.

PREPARING AND POLISHING METALS.

Cast Iron Work.—Such as stove, grate and fender work, which is not intended to be plated.

If the casting is very dirty it is advisable to first immerse in a pickle composed of six fluid ounces of sulphuric acid and one gallon of water to remove all the scale, after which it should be thoroughly rinsed in cold water made alkaline, so as to neutralize any of the acid that is left in the pores ; then proceed to rough up on a Leather Covered Wood Wheel, Buff Leather, Solid Bullneck or Canvas Wheel, running 1600 to 2000 revolutions per minute, coated with No. 60 emery, unless the casting is a very poor one, when it should first be ground down on a grind stone or solid emery wheel ; after roughing up with No. 60 emery, fine with No. 90, and then finish with No. 150 emery.

To set up or coat a wood wheel with emery, first cover with glue and then roll the wheel in emery until the face is entirely covered with the emery, and then it should be set aside to dry, when it is ready for use.

Cast Iron Work.—Which is to be plated, such as pistol or stove work. Rough up with Nos. 80, 120 and flour emery as described in preceding paragraph. Then use a glaze wheel made with Patent Emery Compound for finishing and coloring.

A glaze wheel for this kind of work is either a Leather Covered Wood Wheel, Bullneck, Buff Leather or Felt Wheel prepared as follows : first apply oil to the wheel by means of a roll rag or a daub and then Patent Emery Compound while the wheel is in motion.

Brass Castings.—Dry-faced or Chandelier work. Put in a pickle (about 5 quarts of oil of vitriol to 10 gallons of water) and leave in over night. This cleans out the dirt which is left in the casting. (Only use the pickle when castings are extremely dirty and rough.) Then dip in regular dipping acid, ($\frac{1}{4}$ nitric to $\frac{3}{4}$ sulphuric acid,) rinse in water thoroughly, and dry. Rough up on a Leather Covered Wood Wheel, Bullneck, Walrus Canvas or Felt Wheel, depending upon the work, coated with No. 80 emery, then with No. 120 emery; finish with flour emery and grease on a Leather Covered Wood Wheel, or Patent Emery Compound on a bleached buff, revolving 1,600 to 2,500 revolutions per minute. Cut down or polish with Crocus Composition B, A, BB or FF or Tripoli Composition XXXX, Acme X or R on an unbleached wheel, revolving 2500 to 3000 revolutions per minute. If tubular work, use our Patent Piece Sewed Buff. If matted work, wash the composition out with 381 Cleaning Compound ($\frac{1}{2}$ lb. to 1 gallon of hot water,) rinse in hot water and dry in boxwood sawdust. Color up with CCCC, SSSS, SSS, SS, or SXXXX Hard Rouge, depending on finish required, on an unbleached or Canton flannel wheel, revolving 2,500 to 3,000 revolutions per minute. Then for an extra fine finish which is wanted on fine work, such as chandelier work, wash out the rouge with 681 Cleaning Compound, rinse in hot water, then dry in boxwood sawdust. Dry buff with Hard Rouge on Canton flannel wheel, revolving 2,500 to 3,000 revolutions per minute.

Green Sand Work.—Steamboat and plumber's fittings, etc. Pickle and dip same as for dry sand castings (if very dirty and rough, but it is not necessary unless very dirty,) rough up first with a Leather Covered Wood

Wheel or Bullneck, Canvas or Felt Wheel coated with No. 80 emery, revolving 1,600 to 2,000 revolutions per minute, fine with same kind of wheels coated with 120 emery and finish with our Patent Emery Compound on a bleached buff. Cut down or polish with our Tripoli Composition on an unbleached wheel, revolving 2,500 to 3,000 revolutions per minute. Color up on Canton flannel or unbleached muslin wheel revolving 2,500 to 3,000 revolutions per minute with our Hard Rouge CCCC, SSSS or SSS, depending on the finish required.

Oil Work.—Brass, Copper, etc. Cut down with composition, such as our Tripoli XXXX or Acme X or Crocus B or BB on our Patent White Buff, running 2500 to 3,000 revolutions per minute. Color on an unbleached wheel with Hard Rouge CCCC or SSSS.

To wash out compositions, rouge, grease and dirt from articles, use for large brass, copper, iron and steel work our No. 381 Cleaning Compound (dissolve ½ lb. in one gallon of hot water ;) for brass, German silver, etc., use 681 C. C. (dissolve ½ lb. to one gallon of hot water).

Brittania Metal, Sheet Brass and Sheet Copper.— Sand buff with pumice stone and oil on our Sand Buffing Compound, using No. 1. or No. 2 pumice, depending on roughness of the metal. This to be used on a Walrus, Bullneck or Buff Leather Wheel running 2,500 to 3,000 revolutions per minute. Brass and Copper work can then be finished and colored as described above, whereas Brittania Metal is finished and ready to plate after sand buffing.

CHAPTER IX.

CLEANING METALS FOR NICKEL PLATING.

The success of all kinds of electro-plating depends upon the work being chemically clean, that is free from all grease and dirt. This especially applies to Nickel-Plating, as the chemical character of a nickel solution is such that it has no dissolving action on grease, etc., and the deposit will surely strip or peel from the greasy spots. The operation of cleaning the articles differ in many establishments, but the following methods are those which have been found best from practical experience.

Copper, Brass, Brittania Metal, Tin and Pewter.--
1. Steep the work in a boiling solution of Potash or Salicornia Lye for a few minutes to remove grease and dirt. The stronger the solution the less time it is necessary to leave the work in. To make the solution, dissolve 4 to 8 ozs. of Salicornia Lye in one gallon of water in a kettle, and keep boiling hot.

2. Rinse well in hot water.

3. Dip in cyanide of potash solution, made by dissolving ½ lb. of fused cyanide in one gallon of water. This is to remove any oxydation that may have been formed on the work.

4. Rinse well, first in hot and then in cold water, so that all the potash and cyanide is thoroughly removed from the work, as none must on any account get in the solution, noticing if the water wets the whole surface of the work and runs off without running from

some parts of the work only, as it does with anything that is greasy. If this is the case the work has been properly cleaned ; if not, dip in potash and cyanide and rinse as before. then hang at once in the solution without at any time touching the work with the fingers, as the grease from the fingers will adhere to the work.

Tin, Brittania metal and pewter should not be left long in the lye and cyanide solutions, as those solutions exert a solvent action on tin and its alloys. Hence have strong solutions of both, and only leave in a few seconds.

Steel Articles.—

1.   Steep in the potash or Salicornia Lye solution.
2.   Rinse in hot water.
3.   Scour with pumice.
4.   Rinse in cold water.
5.   Dip for a moment in dilute muriatic acid (muriatic acid one quart, water four quarts.)
6.   Again rinse thoroughly in cold water.
7.   Rinse in lime water (if the work is porous, otherwise it is not necessary) and again in clean cold water, and then hang in the nickel solution. Some platers use oxalic acid in place of muriatic acid, one pound of oxalic acid to one gallon of water. It is a good p'an to have a hot cyanide dip to use on steel work, particularly case-hardened work.

Cast Iron.

1.   Steep in potash or Salicornia Lye as before.
2.   Rinse in water as before
3.   Let the article remain for some time in a pickle composed of sulphuric acid, viz., 4 quarts sulphuric acid to 10 gallons of water. This is partially to dissolve and remove scale.

4. Dip for a moment in dilute muriatic acid, as before.

5. Rinse in water as before.

6. Rinse in lime water (if the work is porous, otherwise it is not necessary) and again in clean cold water and then hang in the nickel solution. Some platers use oxalic acid in place of muriatic acid, one pound of oxalic acid to one gallon of water. It is a good plan to have a hot cyanide dip to use on steel work, particularly case-hardened work.

To Prepare Iron and Stove Trimmings for Nickel Plating.—

1. When first from the "sand," if the casting has considerable background or deadwork, place in a pickle of one quart sulphuric acid and one quart water, from $\frac{1}{2}$ to to 1 minute (or longer if required), then rinse off at once in clear cold water, then put in a hot solution of potash or Salicornia Lye, $\frac{1}{2}$ lb. to 1 gallon of water (keep hot), rinse off in boiling water and dry at once.

2. The casting must then undergo a thorough scratching by sand blast if possible, or by a revolving wheel of flat steel wire, until the casting has the appearance of having been polished with black lead; then take to solid emery wheels and give the flat work a smooth surface; then take a Leather Covered Wood Wheel, Bullneck or Walrus Wheel coated with No. 90 Emery and rough up; then use same kind of wheel coated with No. 120 Emery for fining, then finish or color on canvas or felt glaze wheel charged with Patent Emery Compound until you have a good finish, all scratches being removed; then place in hot potash or Salicornia Lye solution for five minutes ($\frac{1}{2}$ lb. to 1 gallon of water); take from lye and scour with F or O pumice stone, rinse in

cold water and dip in a pickle of one quart sulphuric acid, 12 quarts water, one or two seconds ; thoroughly rinse in cold water ; then dip in lime water, which will kill any acid that may be left in the pores of the article (if the article is very porous) ; then it is necessary to rinse in perfectly clean water, by doing which you will avoid much trouble and peeled work. The last rinsing water should at all times be chemically clean ; then place the work in nickel bath to plate. When a sufficient deposit has been obtained, take work out of bath and rinse thoroughly in cold water, then in hot water, and dry in boxwood sawdust as rapidly as possible ; the work is then taken to the buffing wheel (unbleached muslin wheel is the best) using Patent White Polish, which will finish the work much better than anything else; then immerse in hot solution of No. 381 Cleaning Compound (½ lb. to one gallon of hot water) ; rinse off in hot water and dry in sawdust.

CHAPTER X.

NICKEL=PLATING.

Nickel-Plating is one of the most successful and extensive branches of electro deposition. Realizing the want of a practical treatise on the subject, we take pleasure in supplying the following to our patrons, knowing it to be practical in every detail, and we may say that everything herein embodied has been practically demonstrated in our nickel-plating testing room.

Double Sulphate Solution :—This solution, which is almost universally used, is composed of nickel salts (sulphate of nickel, sulphate of ammonia and water), and is made by dissolving $\frac{3}{4}$lb. of nickel salts to one gallon of boiling water ; when cold, place it in a wooden tank lined with asphaltum or pitch.

Anodes :—After the solution is in the tank, place in the anodes. To insure good plating and to keep the solution in good order the anodes should be placed on both sides of the work on nickel hooks and suspended from a copper or brass tube or rod. Some put anodes only on one side of the work but this is not advantageous and is poor economy, as will be explained further on. Others place anodes crosswise and others again have three rows of anodes and two rows of work.

Connecting Anodes and Work with the Dynamo: —The rod or rods upon which the anodes are suspended should be connected with the positive pole of the dynamo or electric battery by means of a suitable copper wire, and the rod to contain the work must be connected with the negative pole of the machine or battery with a similar wire.

Having everything ready for work we must know, before going further, "What takes place in the Nickel Solution during electrolysis." Nothing is of greater importance to the nickel-plater than to know what is going on in his nickel solution, for otherwise if his solution gets out of order he will spoil it by adding something to it that, had he known what takes place in the bath, he never would have done.

During electrolysis both the sulphate of nickel and the sulphate of ammonia undergo decomposition, sulphuric acid and ammonia being set free at the anode; this sulphuric acid forms an equivalent quantity of sulphate of nickel by its action on the anode which it dissolves ; free ammonia is liberated, some of which is left to accumulate ; this will make the solution decidedly alkaline in time ; and the more intense the electric current the more rapid the decomposition, hence the more ammonia is liberated and the more alkaline the solution becomes, and if this current is too intense, the solution will become too alkaline, which will more or less influence the quality of the work. Accompanying this change in the solution, especially with an irregular or too intense current, there is a precipitation of the nickel in the form of basic salt, by which the metallic strength of the bath is impaired. This necessitates the addition of fresh nickel salts from time to time. Hydrogen and nickel is given up at the cathode, the nickel being deposited on the work and most of the hydrogen liberated, which makes the deposit brittle and strip, especially if the nickel is deposited thick. This is owing to the hydrogen being taken up by the electro deposited metal.

Knowing, from what precedes, what occurs in the bath during electrolysis, we will look into "What is necessary for the proper working of the Solution."

Electric Current.—If this is properly regulated, neither too intense nor too weak, and uniformly maintained, namely, a current of moderate intensity (about two volts), only just enough ammonia will be liberated to combine with the sulphuric acid forming sulphate of ammonia, therefore the difficulty of the solution becoming alkaline is reduced to a minimum.

The deposit of nickel on the work should be tenacious and adherent, and a point to be remembered is, that the slower the rate of deposition the more adherent and tenacious the deposit will be ; but if the current is too weak the deposition will be too slow, and also the solution may crystallize on the anodes. whilst on the other hand if the current is too intense the deposit is apt to burn, that is, the metal deposited will be a dark gray or black color, with a rough surface ; hence, to work the solution properly, a moderately intense and uniform current must be used.

Anode Surface.—A large anode surface should be employed, for nickel is so difficultly soluble that if the anode surface is not considerably larger than the objects to be deposited upon, the solution will not be kept up in strength, for more nickel will be deposited on the work than is dissolved by the sulphuric acid, which is one of the component parts of the double sulphate nickel solution, and the solution will in time contain a great deal of sulphate of ammonia and very little sulphate of nickel, thereby weakening it in nickel and making it acid, owing to too much ammonia being liberated into the air and free sulphuric acid being left in

the solution. Another reason for a large anode surface
is that nickel solutions are feebler conductors of electricity than either gold, silver or copper. On this account
it is necessary to employ a stronger depositing solution and
a larger anode surface to make up for the want of conductivity.

It has been found by practical demonstration that
even though the tank has the ordinary anodes as close
as possible on both sides of the work, there was not
sufficient surface to supply the bath with the proper
amount of nickel to keep up its metallic strength without
the frequent addition of nickel salts. This defect has
been overcome by the use of our

Patent Corrugated Nickel Anodes:—These anodes,
on account of their large surface, supply the bath with
almost as much nickel as is deposited upon the work, and

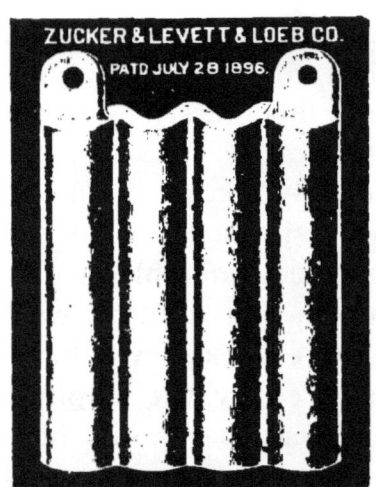

Figure 19.

therefore the metallic strength of the bath is kept up to
the proper standard without the frequent addition of
nickel salts. This not only proves a great saving in the

end, but also prevents the bath becoming saturated with sulphate of ammonia, which is one of the principal ingredients of double nickel salts.

Also, as there is less resistance, an electric current of low voltage (about 1.3 to 1.5 volts) can be used, and the deposition is just as rapid, if not more so, than when a higher voltage is used with the ordinary flat anodes. Moreover, the great advantage in using a low voltage is that the amount of hydrogen given off at the cathode is reduced to a minimum, so that it is not taken up by the deposit. The amount of ammonia given off at the anodes is sufficient to combine with some of the sulphuric acid, also given off at the anodes, to form sulphate of ammonia, this being sufficient to keep the solution properly saturated. There is no excess of ammonia given off which would in time make the solution alkaline.

Owing to the low voltage required, the nickel is not precipitated as basic salts, the addition of nickel salts to the solution thus being avoided.

The gases evolved at the anode with the ordinary anodes shoot straight across to the cathode, thus affecting the deposit on the cathode and making same brittle. With the Patent Corrugated Nickel Anodes, these gases shoot diagonally from the same, strike each other a short distance from them, and come to the surface before reaching the cathode. This is a very important point, and helps the deposit materially.

Difficulties Encountered in Working Nickel Solutions, and their Remedies.—1. The solution may become too alkaline, which may be caused by the electric current being too intense, or insufficient anode surface. The remedy for this is to neutralize the solution, which can be done in two ways ; first, by adding sulphuric acid, drop by drop, until, after stirring the solution and testing with blue litmus paper, the paper turns to a dark purple color when dry. This method of neutralizing the solution is very good, provided the solution is rich in metal. But if the solution is weak in metal, add single salts (Sulphate of Nickel), to the solution until it is neutral, testing with blue litmus paper as above. This being an acid salt of nickel, tends to neutralize the solution, and at the same time adds to the metallic strength of same. If, in order to obtain this neutral condition, you should add such a quantity of single salts as to make the solution too rich in metal, it may be reduced to the proper strength by adding water.

2. The solution may become too acid; in that case add ammonia drop by drop, stir and test with litmus paper until the solution becomes neutral. If then a brown slimy precipitate forms after a short time (which can be determined by putting a little of the stirred solution in a glass and letting it stand for about half an hour) the solution must be filtered, preferably through canton flannel. This acidity occurs principally in plating iron and steel, for these being so sensitive to acid may hold a minute quantity from the pickle which is employed in cleaning the work, and when placed in the bath imparts this acid to it. This is the reason the work is rinsed in lime water after coming out of the pickle, as mentioned in chapter on preparing metals. Most nickel platers prefer to have their solutions slightly acid, but great care must be taken to not get it too much so, because it impairs the working qualities of the solutions.

3. The work may burn; this, as has been remarked, is owing to the current being too intense; to remedy this cut down the current by means of a switchboard.

4. The deposit may be dark in color instead of almost silver-white ; this is caused by the solution being too weak in metal. In this case add single nickel salts (which must first be dissolved in boiling water and allowed to get cold) to the solution to enrich it. If this makes the solution acid, neutralize with ammonia, and test with the hydrometer until the solution stands from 5 to 8 degrees Beaume. This trouble may also be caused by using impure anodes or getting potash or some foreign matter in the bath, or by its being too alkaline.

"Pitting" of the Work in Nickel Plating.—

5. This is a phenomenon, the cause of which, up to the present time it has been difficult to determine. Many theories have been advanced regarding this, the clearest being, that certain gases, developed in nickel plating, remain upon the article in the form of small bubbles, which prevent the nickel from depositing under them, leaving small pin-holes on the work, when the deposition is finished; or dirt settling upon the articles may likewise produce the same effect.

This "pitting" occurs principally on steel or iron work, sometimes appearing at the top of the article, sometimes at the side, and sometimes at the bottom, and will at times occur even though the article is coppered before being nickel plated.

This happens principally in a nickel solution, which is somewhat acid, and is also apt to occur in a solution that is weak in metal. The only remedy for this is to add single salts (sulphate of nickel) to the solution, at first about one pound to every ten gallons of solution. Should this not stop the "pitting" (after, of course, neutralizing the solution with ammonia, filtering the precipitate from the solution, if one forms) then add more single salts. This must be continued until the "pitting" stops, of course keeping the solution at the proper degree Beaume by adding water and keeping it neutral if it should get acid by means of ammonia.

6. The solution may crystallize on the bottom or sides of the tank or on the anodes, or on all three; this is owing to the solution being too concentrated, the plating room being too cold, or a very weak current. Take the crystals all out of the tank and from the anodes, dissolve them in hot water, put this solution in the tank and test with a hydrometer, and dilute until it shows from 5 to 8 degrees Beaume, then see that your electric current is all right.

7. The nickel may precipitate in the form of basic salt from too intense current and by the solution becoming too alkaline. Dissolve the basic salts in boiling water, and put back in the tank; then if the solution is too alkaline add single salts, first dissolving same.

8. By using impure salts and anodes (as those containing copper,) the copper may get in the solution and deposit on the work, making it reddish. To determine whether there is any copper in the solution, fill a glass vessel with the solution and run sulphuretted hydrogen gas into it, making the solution first acid with sulphuric acid. If a dark brown precipitate forms, copper is in the solution, and in that case the whole solution should be treated in the same way, then filter and boil until all the sulphuretted hydrogen is expelled, and neutralize again with ammonia.

Apparatus for making Sulphuretted Hydrogen Gas.—An easy and simple way to make a sulphuretted hydrogen apparatus is to take a wide mouth bottle with an ordinary cork; through the cork insert two glass tubes, one of which should be funnel shaped at the top and should reach within about one half-inch of the bottom of the bottle ; the other should only reach about one half-inch below the cork. This latter tube is connected to a glass tube by a piece of rubber tubing. The above completes a cheap and at the same time practical apparatus for making sulphuretted hydrogen.

To make Sulphuretted Hydrogen Gas.--Place a few pieces of sulphide of iron in the bottle ; add water until the bottle is about one quarter full ; then pour sulphuric acid in the funnel shape tube until chemical action takes place in the bottle, care being taken not to have the liquid in the bottle reach the short tube ; place the glass tube which is at the end of the rubber tubing in the solution which is to be tested and the sulphuretted hydrogen gas which is generated in the bottle will pass through the short tube in the bottle or rubber hose and thence into the solution.

Cleaning the Solution.—After a time the solution becomes dirty and the sediment must be got rid of. Some let their solution stand, pour off the clear liquid and throw away the sediment, which also necessitates a certain amount of the solution being thrown away. This is a very bad way of doing, for according to certain laws of liquids the heaviest part of the solution, that is, that containing most metal, after standing, is at the bottom ; hence by throwing that away we throw away the most metallic part of the bath, thus weakening it. Some do not know this and when they find their solution weakened do not know the cause The proper way to clean the solution is to take a piece of board and scrape the sediment to one side and take it out without removing the solution from the tank ; or make a filter of Canton flannel or cotton, and filter the solution through it, and put back into the tank. Test with hydrometer, and if the solution does not stand from 5 to 8 Beaume, add single nickel salts (sulphate of nickel) dissolved in warm water, until you can get the right degree, 5 to 8 Beaume.

Stringing the Work.—It is important to have the wires for supporting the work of a proper gauge. Some do not pay any attention to the importance of this. Small articles require a very thin wire, while larger ones a larger wire; also, owing to the conductivity of the metals, the wire should be larger or finer. Copper, brass and steel articles will be readily plated if suspended by a very fine wire in the solution, whilst lead, Brittania metal, pewter and cast iron would not plate so readily if suspended from the same wire ; hence, the operator must not only be guided by the size of the article, but the metal from which it is made, in selecting his stringing wire. For small articles and metal of the first class use a copper stringing wire 22 to 23 B. & S. gauge, for larger articles of the first class and small articles of second class use a copper wire 16 to 20 B. & S. gauge. Never use an iron wire for stringing work.

Length of Time to Leave the Work in the Bath.-- The time for leaving work in the nickel bath depends upon the strength of the electric current, condition of the bath, conductivity of the metal of which the article is made, and the amount of anode surface. Everything being in the proper condition, as before explained, copper, brass, etc., should remain in the bath from ten minutes to half an hour. A splendid deposit is obtained in 15 minutes. Iron, steel, pewter, Brittania metal, etc., from 20 minutes to one hour ; this is owing to their inferior conductivity.

Special work, such as bicycle parts and other articles exposed to the atmosphere, should be run from 2 to 3 hours according to the thickness of deposit desired. See chapter XII. for special article on Bicycle Plating.

A nickel solution should be stirred every night or morning, otherwise the heaviest and richest part of the solution will be at the bottom, and the work will have a heavier deposit on the lower end than at the top, and in time the bottom of the anodes will be covered with crystals.

Wash water should at all times be chemically clean.

Nickel Plating Direct on Zinc.—We furnish this solution all ready for plating ; it is used the same as the double sulphate solution, except that the work must be connected with the electric current before being placed in the solution.

After Plating.—The work should be taken from the nickel bath and rinsed in cold water, then boiling water, and then dried in hot boxwood sawdust ; then it should be polished on an unbleached muslin buff (running 2500 to 3000 revolutions per minute,) with hard rouge or Patent White Polish, after which it should be steeped in a hot solution of our 381 or 681 Cleaning Compound (½ lb. to 1 gallon of water) if necessary ; then rinsed in cold water, then in hot water, and then dried in hot boxwood sawdust, when it is ready for inspection.

Nickel Hooks.—Heretofore it has been customary to use hooks made of copper for suspending Nickel Anodes in the bath. This is apt to contaminate the solution with copper, as the hooks may dip into the solution and the action of the electric current would dissolve them. Nickel Hooks should be used, which prevents any such possibility.

58

CHAPTER XI.

POLISHING BICYCLE WORK.

In polishing handle bars or other round bent parts of a bicycle, endless belts and sheepskin or soft bullneck and walrus wheels are used. For cranks and other straight or flat parts, hard bullneck or leather covered wood wheels are used.

These are set up first with No. 90 Emery for roughing, then with No. 120 Emery for fining, and with Flour Emery for finishing. After these parts are polished on the above, they are greased on felt grease wheels, that is, felt wheels set up with flour emery worn smooth and then greased or oiled, or a felt wheel of medium hardness with our Patent Emery Compound.

In some cases Patent Piece Printers Ink Buffs can be used with the Patent Emery Compound for the same purpose, and will give a fine finish.

In this connection we think it advisable to give another method of grinding and polishing iron and steel work, which practically has also been found to give excellent results.

First grind or cut down the work on a leather covered wood wheel charged with No. 60 or No. 90 Emery, and for finishing use a very soft wheel, such as a buff leather or walrus, bullneck or felt wheel, charged with No. 120 or No. 150 Emery.

If No. 60 Emery is used for cutting down, set the wheel for finishing with No. 120 Emery, but if No. 90 Emery is used for cutting down, set the wheel for finishing with No. 150 Emery. Work the wheel down to a smooth surface, then rub or charge the wheel well with bayberry tallow, and work down to a smooth surface before using it on the work, or use a felt wheel charged with our Patent Emery Compound.

Though we have given two different ways of doing the work, the first gives the better finish.

If a very high finish is desired for bicycle parts before plating, it is advisable to use the wheel set up with a mixture of flour emery and glue, the operation of finishing being the same as with the No. 120 or No. 150 Emery.

To prepare the flour emery and glue mixture, make the glue only half the usual consistency, then add a sufficient quantity of flour emery to make the mass the usual consistency of glue, and apply to the wheel with a brush when very hot ; let wheel dry hard before using. Make but little at a time, as it soon spoils.

In polishing tubular work, such as handle bars, etc., use first the Endless Polishing Belt set in No. 70 to No. 100 Emery. To finish, use walrus wheels varying in width from ¾″ to 1¼″ thickness and 3″ to 5″ diameter. Turn the wheel concave enough to let the work slide easily in the groove.

In finishing handle bars, and in fact the whole frame, when it is plated, it is much better to polish the tubing lengthwise, which is the reason we mention concave wheels. Some manufacturers, however, polish them crosswise, in which case use flat face wheels.

CHAPTER XII.

NICKEL PLATING BICYCLE PARTS.

Bicyle parts after being polished are taken to the plating room. When nickel is deposited direct on iron or steel, and exposed to the air, the iron or steel is apt to rust through the plating. Therefore it is much better to copper-plate all such articles before nickel plating, which prevents rusting to a considerable extent and improves the finish.

The articles are first wired or put on racks or pieces of wire bent in such a way as to hold them securely in the solution.

They are then immersed in a hot solution of Salicornia Lye for from 10 to 15 minutes. This will remove all the grease or oil. They are then thoroughly rinsed in cold water and scoured with fine pumice stone, using a plater's brush. They are again rinsed in water and then dipped into an acid dip, composed of about one pint of muriatic acid to one gallon water, or of one pound oxalic acid to one gallon of water. This will remove any oxide that may have been formed on the articles. They are again rinsed in cold water, then put in hot cyanide of potassium dip, again rinsed in clean cold water, and are at once placed or suspended in the copper solution and are plated from 5 to 20 minutes, according to the thickness of the deposit required and the strength of the electric current used. When plated in a hot copper solution they are only left in from $\frac{1}{2}$ to 1 minute.

If the copper solution is used cold, and the articles

have a heavy deposit, they are then rinsed in cold water, then plunged in boiling water, then dried in boxwood sawdust, and are afterwards removed to the buffing room, where they are colored on an unbleached muslin buff with Patent White Polish or SSS or SSSS rouge, and are then returned to the plating room to be nickel-plated. They are again wired up as before, placed in the solution of hot Salicornia Lye for a few minutes, to remove the dirt and grease from the buffing operation, again rinsed in cold water, and are this time brushed with whiting, then thoroughly rinsed in water, dipped in a weak solution of cyanide of potassium to remove any oxidization or tarnish. They are then rinsed in cold water and placed at once in the nickel solution.

When a hot copper solution is used and the articles are only slightly coated with copper, they are thoroughly rinsed in cold water and then placed immediately in the nickel solution, which does away with all the extra work of repolishing and recleaning.

They remain in the nickel solution from one to three hours, depending on the thickness of the deposit required. They are then removed from the nickel solution, rinsed thoroughly in cold water, plunged in boiling water and dried in hot boxwood sawdust. They are then taken to the buffing room and are finished or colored up on a soft buff, usually an unbleached muslin buff, with Patent White Polish.

The above is the most improved method of plating bicycle parts, and is used in the largest bicycle factories in the United States, and the results obtained have been very satisfactory. Great care must be exercised in all these operations.

A low intensity of current, say about $1\frac{1}{2}$ to 2 volts, should be employed, the solutions should stand from 5 to 8 Beaume, and as large an anode surface as possible should be used in order to obtain a deposit which is white in color, malleable, adherent and nonporous.

A large anode surface is best obtained by using our Patent Corrugated Nickel Anodes, (See chapter X. on Nickel Plating).

CHAPTER XIII.

COPPER PLATING.

Cleaning theWork.—Same as for nickel (see page 43)

Setting up the Bath.—Same as for nickel (see page 47)

Working the Bath.—All good copper plating is done with cyanide solutions, with the exception of electrotyping. All articles made of brass, German silver, spelter, etc., can be given a good deposit in fifteen minutes, whereas articles made of iron and steel should be run twenty to thirty minutes, depending upon the thickness required. If the work is properly prepared and cleaned, a copper solution is very easy to manage and does not readily get out of order.

Finishing the Work.—The work on being taken from the solution should be immediately rinsed thoroughly in cold water, then in hot water, and then dried in hot boxwood sawdust, as in nickel, and then polished with SSSS or SSS hard rouge, depending on the finish required.

Caution to be Observed.—When the anodes have a greenish scum on them, the solution is not rich enough in cyanide, and the scum will retard the passage of the current ; therefore, add 2 to 4 ozs. of C. P. cyanide to the gallon of solution. Never use fused cyanide, as its impurities may injure the solution. The solution may refuse to plate although the anodes have no greenish scum ; in that case put on the current and see if the solution boils vigorously around the work (there will, however, always be a slight boiling, even if the solution is all right); if it does boil vigorously, there is too much cyanide in the solution, and it dissolves the metal as soon as deposited and prevents plating. In this case add metal to the solution, which can be done by the addition of Carbonate of Copper (boil the solution after adding) or by hanging an Iron Cathode in the solution and letting it work with the full current for a couple of hours, using the regular anodes. Then try to plate. If it plates properly there is then enough metal in the solution. If the solution works slowly, as it will after a time when it gets too rich in metal, add 2 to 4 ozs. of C. P. Cyanide per gallon. A blue colored solution will never plate good--it has not enough cyanide. The color of a solution, to do good work, should be a light yellowish, resembling old ale.

CHAPTER XIV.

BRONZE PLATING.

It is difficult to obtain a bronze solution that will work cold and which is always reliable. As different shades of bronze plating is often desired, the solution should be made in two parts, one red, the other white, thereby giving the plater a chance to regulate the solution according to the color of bronze desired, which is accomplished as follows : Take all the red solution (which call.No. 1), place it in the tank ; add, say one-quarter of the white solution (which call No 2); stir them, place in the anodes. and plate. Keep adding the white solution until the desired shade of plating is obtained. It must be understood that the white solution mentioned here is much different to the white solution mentioned under the head of Brass Plating, and one must not be used in place of the other.

Cleaning the Work.—Same as for nickel, extreme care being requisite with iron and steel that all the scale, rust and plumbago of the facing of the moulds in cast iron is removed, and the surface to be plated is uniformly clean. Great caution is necessary with regard to this, otherwise the plating will be redder in color in places not clean than in the clean places. To get proper colored plating the electric current necessary to use is from 4 to 8 volts, depending upon the kind of metal that is being plated, but should you not then obtain the desired results, add either some of the white or red solution, as the case may require, to the main solution until you btain the correct color. The proper regulation of the solution and the electric current is of the utmost importance, without which bronze plating cannot be successfully accomplished.

Working the Solution.—Place the work in the bath, switch on the electric current, watch if the color is satisfactory, and after properly regulating the current, let it plate on said current for the length of time required; then, before removing any of the work from the bath, cut off the current; otherwise, by taking some of the work out, and before you get out the rest, those taken out last will be of a lighter color, being subjected to a more intense current. This is absolutely important.

Caution to be Observed.—The anodes may have a greenish scum; in that case do the same as in copper plating (see page 63); also, if the solution works slow. The proper color for a bronze solution is a straw color; otherwise it will never be a good working solution. The anodes should be a pure bronze, and exactly the shade of the plating required, or the solution will, after a time, plate the color of the metal of the anode, as that is the metal which feeds the solution. If the solution plates two or three different colors on the same piece of work, at the same time, the work being chemically clean and the current of the proper intensity, the solution is useless and should be discarded.

Finishing the Work.—Finish on an unbleached muslin wheel running 2200 to 2500 revolutions, using Hard Rouge SSSS or SSS. Wash dirt out of filagree work with 681 cleaning compound (½ pound to 1 gallon hot water).

CHAPTER XV.

BRASS PLATING.

No solution is so troublesome to manage as brass. As different shades of brass plating is often desired, the solution should be made in two parts, one red and the other white, thereby giving the plater a chance to regulate the solution according to the color of brass desired, which is accomplished as follows: Take all the red solution (No. 1), place it in the tank; add about one-quarter of the white solution (No. 2); stir them and place the anodes in the solution, and then plate. Keep adding the white solution until the desired shade of plating is obtained.

Cleaning the Work.—(See Bronze), page 65.

Proper Colored Plating.—(See Bronze), page 65.

Working the Solution.—Brass, iron, steel, spelter, etc., cannot be plated at the same time in the same bath, for an alloy of copper and zinc must be deposited at the same time, and copper being of different resistance from zinc, will deposit on the easiest metal and carry the zinc with it, so that if copper and iron are the two metals in the bath, the copper will get all the plating and the iron none. Wrought and cast iron act the same; also zinc and iron and any dissimilar metals. When iron screws, buckles, or other small articles are to be plated in a basket, it is best to have the basket of the same metal as the articles. In plating iron articles in a brass bath, it sometimes happens that they will show (after plating, say 20 minutes) reddish streaks, in which case the article must be removed from the bath, rinsed in hot water, dried in sawdust, scratch-brushed, replaced in the bath and left for about 5 to 10 minutes longer, when the color should be beautiful and uniform, and without streaks. This is very important. Should some parts of the work be of a redder color than other parts, the red parts are not clean and must be made so, because copper, being so much easier to deposit than zinc, will deposit on even a slightly dirty surface, and the zinc will not ; hence you get the reddish color.

Some claim that after a short time the solution will plate a redder color than at first, owing to the zinc oxide which forms on the anodes not being dissolved by the cyanide and other ingredients of the solution, and recommend chemicals, such as arsenic, etc., as a remedy. We may here say, if the solution is properly made and pure brass anodes are used, the plating will remain the same color as long as the solution lasts. Scouring with sea sand after plating does a great deal of good in making the plating bright. It is, however, often found advantageous to suspend a small copper tube from the cathode rod into the solution while there is no work in the bath and if the electric current is on, for by doing so it will help to keep the zinc oxide from forming on the anodes.

If a solution plates reddish, greenish, brassy and whitish at the same time, on the same piece of work, the solution is useless.

Never try to "doctor" a solution, for the more you add to it the more complicated you get it and the worse it will work.

Some platers copper their articles before brassing. This is a good plan, but of course adds to the cost and is not essential.

Example No. 1 —

If you have a copper article to brass plate, size about 1" x 2", proceed as follows :

String on a No. 23 copper wire (for a larger piece of work a heavier wire—see Nickel), then dip in hot potash or Salicornia lye solution for a minute, rubbing with the potash brush ; then rinse in hot water, then in cold water, then dip for an instant in cold cyanide of potassium solution, then in hot water, then in cold water, and immediately, without letting the article touch anything or handling it, place in the bath and turn on the electric current, and after properly regulating the same, let plate. After being in from 10 to 20 minutes, cut off the current, take out the work, rinse in cold water, then in hot water, and then place in hot boxwood sawdust. When dry, finish or polish with SS or SSS Rouge on unbleached muslin buff (see Polishing), and then dip in 681 cleaning compound solution, then in hot water, and then dry in sawdust as above, and lacquer.

Example No. 2—

If you have a cast iron article to brass plate, size about 2"x3", proceed as follows :

String as in example No. 1, then place in a pickle composed of sulphuric acid, 4 ozs. to 1 gallon of cold water, leave in for ½ hour ; this will loosen all scale and rust ; then rinse in cold water, then scour with pumice and rinse in cold water, place in the solution and plate as before, only leaving in from 15 to 25 minutes, and finish as in example No. 1.

Example No. 3.—

For articles less than 1" x 2", and which it is not

economical to plate by stringing.   These must be plated in a wire basket of same metal as articles to be plated, after first cleaning properly, or tumbled in a tumbling barrel.   Finish as in example No. 1.

CHAPTER XVI.

SILVER PLATING.

Providing the solution is made properly, silver is the easiest of all metals to deposit. We have found by experience that the best silver solutions are made with cyanide of potassium and chloride of silver, but both of these must be chemically pure. In silver plating a large anode surface is not necessary, as good plating can be done with almost any size within reason. Always take anodes out of solution when not in use, otherwise the action of the cyanide in the solution will dissolve them even though the electric current is not on, thereby making the solution too rich in metal.

Cleaning the Work.—Same as for nickel plating. Before plating such metals as brass, copper, Brittania, etc., it is best to use what is called in the trade a blue dip, which is composed of ½ oz. of bi-chloride of mercury, 6 ozs. of muriate of ammonia (sal-ammoniac) and two gallons of water, and which is used as follows: After cleaning the article as described under nickel plating, immerse it in the blue dip, rinse in clean water, and then place in the silver solution.

Striking Solution.—For such articles as steel knives, forks, etc., a "striking solution" should be used. A striking solution is rich in cyanide and poor in silver, about 10 or 12 ozs. of cyanide and ½ oz. silver chloride to the gallon. A strong electric current should be employed and a large silver anode used. After cleaning the work as in nickel plating, immerse it in a weak muriatic acid dip, composed of 1 oz. of muriatic acid to a gallon of water, then rinse in clean cold water and put it in the "striking solution," where it is left for about one minute, after which it is at once placed in the regular silver solution, where it remains until the desired thickness of deposit is obtained.

The above method is the best and most economical where the work is done in a large way, but it is not absolutely necessary in a small plant. The electric current employed for the regular silver solution should be from ¾ to 1½ volts. The current should be on while the articles are being placed in the solution and should be regulated by a switchboard, so as to increase the intensity as more articles are put in.

The amount of silver deposited can be determined by weight. The thickness of an ordinary piece of writing paper corresponds to from 1¼ to 1½ ozs. of silver to the square foot of surface, and is considered a very good coating. A good silvering solution should deposit silver by simple immersion, but very slightly, otherwise the solution has too much free cyanide and the plating is apt to peel or rub off. Should the solution, on the other hand, plate too slowly, it is too rich in metal and has not enough cyanide. It is best to copper iron and zinc work before silvering.

In a great many of the largest silver plating establishments in the country, the following method is used on steel knives, forks, etc., for striking : A solution rich in cyanide and weak in metal, (about 1½ lbs. of cyanide and from ½ to 1 oz. chloride of silver to the gallon,) is used, into which is placed small silver and large copper anodes, the propotionate size being about four to one, and a strong electric current is employed.

Finishing Silver Plated Articles.—After the articles

have received a sufficient deposit, they should be removed from the rod one at a time, swilled for a moment in the plating solution, allowed to drain, rinsed well in clean hot water and dried in clean hot boxwood sawdust. If they should be yellow or spotty after drying, the cause may be traced to imperfect rinsing or to the use of dirty sawdust. After they are dry, they should be scratch-brushed until the white "burr" or "matt" is worked down, the scratch-brush being kept wet all the time with stale beer. After scratch-brushing. they are rinsed in clean water, again dried in sawdust, and are ready for the finishing process. Then they should be colored or finished on a Canton flannel buff, using hard rouge, SS, S or SXXXX, depending on the fineness of finish desired.

Burnishing.—Such articles as spoons, forks, trays and other plated table ware are burnished to give them a very highly polished mirror-like surface. Burnishing is done by means of polished steel tools or tools faced with agate or bloodstone, which are pressed on the surface of the plated art'cle and rubbed to and fro until the desired polish is obtained. After being scratch-brushed and dried in sawdust, the articles are prepared for burnishing by scouring the surface with very fine silver sand, which is applied on a soft flannel pad dipped in warm, soapy water. Then the articles are rinsed in hot water and dried, when they are ready to be burnished. There are numerous shapes of burnishers suitable for different classes of work, the first rough burnishing being often done by instruments with comparatively sharp edges, while the finishing operations are accomplished with rounded ones. The manner of using them has to be acquired by practice, but we may say that they are held in the right hand with the handle resting on the back of the little finger near the first knuckle, the next three fingers on the upper part of the handle and the thumb on the top to apply pressure. In burnishing, the strokes must all be in one direction, and each succeeding stroke should overlap its predecessor. The tool should be held in a slanting direction on the article and only a moderate pressure applied. It is necessary to have near by a vessel containing soapy water into which the burnished article must be dipped from time to time, for it must be kept well lubricated with soap-suds, or it will heat and strip the plating off the article. Thin deposits of silver will not stand much, if any, burnishing.

CHAPTER XVII.

GOLD PLATING.

Gold is a metal that is very easily deposited and there is no other capable of such a variety in the color of its deposit. Solutions and anodes can be bought ready for use to plate any color from a pure gold to a red gold. They are run both hot and cold, depending upon the class of work. The anodes should always be kept out of the solution when not in use, otherwise they will be dissolved by the cyanide in the solution and make it too rich in metal. Should the solution deposit too slowly, C. P. cyanide of potassium should be added, about ½ to 1 oz. to the gallon.

Too much gold in the solution makes the deposit black or dark red, and when too much cyanide is in the solution the deposit will be grayish, and often pieces already gilded lose their deposit.

When the solution is run hot, enamelled iron vessels should be used, but when run cold, glass or porcelain jars can likewise be used.

An electric current of about 1½ to 2 volts should be used for gold plating.

Cleaning the Work.—Same as for nickel plating.

Finishing Gold Plated Articles.—Same as for silver plating.

CHAPTER XVIII.
TIN PLATING.

As most articles are tinned by the molten process, very little attention has been given to the electro-deposition of tin, although this metal can be easily deposited electrically.

Tin solutions should not be used at a temperature below 68 degrees Fahrenheit and they require an electric current of about 2 to 3 volts. Too strong a current causes a pulverulent reduction of the tin. Pure cast tin anodes with as large a surface as possible should be used. As tin solutions do not dissolve the anodes in proportion to the amount of metallic tin drawn from the bath, no matter how large the anodes surface, it is necessary to add from time to time small quantities of tin salts or some concentrated tin solution. This is best done by having suspended over the tank a small vessel containing a concentrated solution of tin, which is allowed to run drop by drop into the tank below. By this means the regular plating solution is kept rich and constant in metal In some cases it is a good plan to first plate iron and steel objects with copper, and after scratch-brushing the copper deposit, place in the tin solution.

The work is cleaned the same as for nickel plating. For heavy deposits of tin the objects are frequently taken from the bath, and the deposit is thoroughly brushed with a brass wire scratch-brush, rinsed in water, and returned to the bath.

When the tinning is finished, the articles are brushed with a brass wire scratch-brush, then dried in hot box-wood sawdust and polished with fine whiting.

CHAPTER XIX.
GALVANOPLASTY.

Electrotyping and Galvanoplasty are very similar branches of the Art of Electro-Deposition ; in fact. the former·is a stepping stone to the latter. As electrotyping proper does not, strictly speaking, come under the heading of electro-plating, we will only treat on it in so far as it is connected with galvanoplasty.

Galvanoplasty consists of reproducing, in copper, various articles of a non-conducting material in an electro-typing solution, or of copper plating in the electrotyping solution the articles themselves, such as leaves, shells, fish, flowers, insects, etc. Small articles are afterwards generally plated with gold or silver, thus forming beautiful objects for ornament.

The Process is as follows.—Free the articles from all dust, grease and dirt, and then apply a slight coat of Diamond Dip Lacquer with a camel's hair brush. Be careful not to miss any of the ornamental depths, parts or corners. Wait about 1 minute, when the lacquer will have become half-dry, (pasty or sticky). Then apply graphite with another camel's hair brush by drawing the graphite loosely over the article. Pound slightly in the deep places and corners, then rub easy until a dark gray lustre is obtained. . Brush all the loose graphite off, being careful to leave none loose in the deep places and corners. Then wrap loosely with thin copper wire, being careful that the wire will not slide over the article ; if it should do so, rub over with graphite. Rinse well in cold water until all loose graphite is removed, then immerse in the electrotyping solution. The article should be coated in about 20 to 30 minutes ; if not, the article is not well covered with graphite. In this case the article must be washed in cold water, well dried, lacquered, covered with graphite and put in the solution again.

An Electrotyping Solution.—To make an Electrotyping or Acid Copper Solution, dissolve about 1½ to 2 lbs. of sulphate of copper to each gallon of water. After the sulphate of copper is all dissolved, the solution should show about 16 degrees Baume Hydrometer, then add sulphuric acid until it shows about 19 degrees Baume. It is important to test the solution from time to time, to see that it shows about this density, and in case it does not, add more sulphate of copper or sulphuric acid.

On the other hand great care must be exercised that the solution does not become too acid or dense, as dark red streaks will show on the back of the shell. The temperature of the solution should always be kept as near 60 degrees Fahrenheit as possible. Pure copper anodes should be used and an electric current of about 1½ to 2 volts employed.

When articles that have gone through the galvanoplastic process are to be plated with other metals, they are cleaned and prepared like any other metal articles, as described in previous chapters.

CHAPTER XX.

DIPS.

Dips are used for oxydizing silver, brass, etc., also for imparting different colors to metals.

Bright Acid Dip.—Composed of oil of vitriol and nitric acid, half-and-half. The work is first dipped in this, then immediately into water, then again into the acid dip, then again into water, continuing this process until the brass is perfectly bright and clean, ending the operation with the water. It must then be thoroughly rinsed in clean water and dried in boxwood sawdust.

Silver Oxydizing Dip.—Dissolve about $\frac{1}{4}$ to $\frac{1}{2}$ lb. of sulphurette of potassium in one gallon of water and use at about 160 degrees Fahrenheit. First scratch-brush the article, then immerse in the dip, rinse in water, and again scratch-brush while still wet If the article is not black enough, repeat the process until the desired effect is obtained, then rinse in hot water, dry in boxwood sawdust and lacquer.

Black Brass Dip—Dissolve $\frac{1}{2}$ lb plastic carbonate of copper in one gallon water. The work, after being properly cleaned, is immersed in this dip, which should be kept at about 150 degrees Fahrenheit, then rinsed in water. This process is continued until the brass is black or of the desired color. The operation should end with the water, and the article immediately dried in boxwood sawdust.

Antique Dip.—Dissolve about $\frac{1}{4}$ to $\frac{1}{2}$ lb. of sulphurette of potassium in one gallon of water. The operation is the same as with black brass dip, with the exception that the dip is run cold.

Ormulo Dip.—This is a dip composed of 1 gallon aquafortis and ½ gallon sulphuric acid ; 2½ lbs sulphate of zinc, ¼ lb. sulphate of copper, ½ oz. sulphur, ¼ oz. white arsenic. Let this boil for ten hours ; use while boiling and rinse in hot potash water. Run through the bright-acid dip. The dip should stand at about 50 degrees Beaume.

Gold Dip.—This gives a beautiful yellow gold color to bright-acid dipped brass and brass plated articles. It is made as follows ; dissolve 5 dwts. of gold chloride in water, precipitate with ammonia, thoroughly wash the precipitate and add it to one gallon water, 2 lbs. yellow prussiate of potash and 2 lbs. sal soda. Boil all together and use at about 150 to 175 degrees Fahrenheit. After the work is dipped in this and becomes gold plated, it should be rinsed in water and dried in hot boxwood sawdust. Parts wanted bright should be burnished.

Bi=Chloride of Platinum Dip.—This is made by dissolving about one ounce of bi-chloride of platinum in one gallon of water and is used for producing a black or steel grey coloration on solid silver and silver plated ware.

Silver Dip.—This gives a light silver deposit to small articles of brass, copper, etc. It is made as follows: one gallon water, ½ lb. C. P. cyanide of potassium, ¾ to one oz. chloride of silver. It is used by simply dipping the articles in it, after they are first thoroughly cleaned or bright-acid dipped.

CHAPTER XXI.
LACQUERING.

Lacquers are used to prevent articles from tarnishing or oxidizing, and likewise for imparting different colors to metals. They are used especially on brass, copper, bronze, silver and all tarnishable metals. They should leave a transparent, clear, bright film, hard and flexible, which cannot be scratched by the finger nail. Colored lacquers are used where a certain color is wanted on the goods. They protect the work the same as the transparent lacquers.

Articles are lacquered by either dipping them in the lacquer or by applying the lacquer to them by means of a camel's hair brush. The work should be perfectly dry and free from grease and dirt of any kind. In the dipping process, the work is immersed in the lacquer, taken out, allowed to drain and hung up to dry. Any number of coats may be put on by simply dipping the articles the required number of times, taking care that each coat is dry before another is applied. In the brushing process, care must be taken not to have the lacquer too thin, as in that event it will produce irridescent colors on the work ; to remedy this, give the work an extra coat.

Lacquers, when not in use, should always be kept covered, otherwise they will congeal and must be brought back to their proper consistency by adding a reducer or thinner.

CHAPTER XXII.

CHEMICALS USED IN PLATING ROOM.

The principal acids used in electro-plating are Sulphuric Acid, (Oil of Vitriol,) Nitric Acid. Muriatic Acid and Aqua Fortis.

Sulphuric Acid.--Is a thick, oily fluid. If pure it is white, but is usually brownish from organic matter. It should stand at 66 degrees Beaume with the hydrometer. In diluting this acid with water, it should in every case be added to the water, and not the water to it, otherwise an explosion might occur from the mixture of the two. This acid is used for pickling and stripping.

Nitric Acid and Aqua Fortis.—36 to 40 degrees should be used. It should be white, but sometimes is more or less yellow. It is used for pickling, stripping and dipping, and is sometimes mixed with sulphuric acid for this purpose. It is also used in the Bunsen and Smee cells. The yellow fumes given off by this acid when dissolving metals should not be inhaled, as they are poisonous.

Muriatic Acid.—When pure it is colorless, but usually is of a yellow color from the presence of iron. It should stand at about 18 degrees Beaume. It is generally used for pickling iron.

Citric Acid. Colorless crystals, which dissolve with great ease in both hot and cold water. It is only used for acidulating nickel baths and in the preparation of platinum baths.

Boracic Acid.—This is in the shape of scales or crystals ; dissolves with difficulty in cold water ; more rapidly soluble in boiling water. It is sometimes used in the nickel bath.

Arsenious Acid or White Arsenic.—This is in the form of a white powder, slightly soluble in cold water and more readily soluble in hot water and hydrochloric acid. It is generally used in brass solutions and for oxidizing copper alloys.

Bichromate of Potash.—This is in the form of orange red crystals and is soluble in water, forming an orange colored liquid, and is used in the bichromate battery.

Caustic Potash or Potassium Hydrate.--This is usually found in commerce, in various degrees of purity, either in sticks or lumps. It is deleqnescent, dissolves readily in water and alcohol. The pure potash is generally used as an addition to zinc and gold baths The commercial article is used for removing grease and dirt from objects to be plated.

Caustic Soda.—It occurs in commerce in sticks and lumps. It is used for removing grease and dirt from objects that are to be plated.

Ammonia Hydrate and Ammonia.—This is water saturated with ammonia gas. It must be stored in closely stoppered bottles, so that this gas is not evolved. 20 degree ammonia is usually employed. It is used for neutralizing nickel solutions when they are too acid, and also used in copper and brass baths. It is recognized by its odor.

Potassium Sulphurett, Liver Sulphur, Sulphide of Potassium.—This is a hard, liver-colored mass, becoming green when exposed to the air. It readily absorbs moisture and is acted upon by the light, which spoils it. It is employed for making oxidizing dips for copper, silver, bronze, etc.

Ammonium Sulphide, Sulphurett of Ammonia, Hydro Sulphide of Ammonia.—When freshly prepared it is a clear, colorless liquid, with the odor of ammonia and sulphuretted hydrogen. It becomes yellow by standing but does not spoil, and is used for the same purpose as sulphurett of potassium.

Carbon Di-Sulphide or Bi-Sulphide.—This is a colorless, transparent liquid, with a very disagreeable odor. It is very volatile and explosive and is used in a bright silver plating solution.

Ferric Sulphide is a hard, black mass, used for making sulphuretted hydrogen gas.

Ammonia Chloride, Salamoniac.—A white substance in the shape of fibrous crystals. It is soluble in about 2¾ parts cold and a much smaller quantity of hot water. It is used for silvering and tinning and is a conducting salt in many solutions.

Copper Chloride.—Blue-green crystals, readily soluble in cold water. It is employed in copper and brass solutions.

Tin Chloride, Tin Salts or Tin Crystals.—White crystalline salts, readily soluble in water, the solution becoming turbid in the air. It is used in making brass, bronze and tin solutions

Zinc Chloride or Muriate of Zinc or Butter of Zinc.—A white crystalline or confused mass, very soluble in water and deliquescent in the air. It is used in making brass and zinc baths, silvering, etc.

Nickel Chloride.—This is in the form of a green or

yellowish mass and is used in the preparation of nickel solution.

Silver Chloride (Horn Silver).—A heavy white powder which is acted upon by the light, gradually passing from purple to black. It is insoluble in water, but dissolves readily in potassium cyanide solution. It is the principal salt employed in making silver plating solutions and is also used in a paste for silvering by friction.

Gold Chloride (Chloride of Gold, Muriate of Gold, Auric Chloride).—This is in the form of crystals, yellow in color or a reddish-brown crystalline mass; it absorbs moisture from the air, becoming a gold colored liquid. It is used principally for making gold solutions.

Platinum Chloride. (Bichloride of Platinum).—In the form of a red-brown mass; very soluble and becomes wet by absorbing moisture from the air when exposed to same. It is used principally for oxidizing silver, brass, etc., and in making platinum solutions for platinum plating.

Potassium Cyanide or Cyanide of Potassium.— This is one of the most important chemicals used in electro-plating. It is made at the present day as near chemically pure as possible. running as high as 98 to 99 per cent. pure. There are also cyanides of 30%, 50%, 60% and 80%. These latter are principally used for cleaning work before plating. The chemically pure cyanide of potassium is used principally in the preparation of copper, brass, silver and gold baths. The pure cyanide of potassium is a white, translucent crystalline mass like lump sugar, the crystalline structure being plainly visible upon fracture. When perfectly dry it is odorless, but when absorbing moisture it has a strong smell of prussic acid. It is very readily soluble in cold water; when dissolved in hot water it is partially decomposed, which is recognized by the odor of ammonia. It is a deadly poison and great care should be exercised in its use. Fused cyanide of potassium, or the lower percentages, which are called commercial, is a white, opaque substance, crystalline upon fracture, absorbing moisture from the air same as the chemically pure. The principal impurity of cyanide of potassium is carbonate of potash; it is readily detected by dilute muriatic acid, when, if the salt is impure, it will effervesce.

Copper Cyanide.—This is a greenish-brown powder used for making electro-plating solutions of copper, brass and red gold.

Zinc Cyanide.—A white powder, insoluble in water; soluble in potassium cyanide, ammonia and alkaline sulphites; it is used principally in the preparation of brass baths.

Silver Cyanide.—A white powder, becoming black when exposed to the light; employed principally in the preparation of silver baths.

Sodium Carbonate. (Sal soda).—It occurs in commerce in large colorless crystals; on exposure to the air effloresces and crumbles to a white powder; dissolves readily in water; is used principally in copper and brass baths, and for cleaning articles.

Sodium Bicarbonate.—A white powder, soluble in water; used for similar purposes as the sal soda above.

Copper Carbonate.—A blue substance, insoluble in water; soluble with effervescence in acids; also in cyanide of potassium; employed principally in making copper, brass, bronze and gold baths, also for removing an excess of acid in sulphate of copper solutions (electrotyper's). It is best used in plastic form for solutions as it thereby dissolves more readily in a cyanide of potassium solution.

Zinc Carbonate.—A white substance, insoluble in water, but soluble in acids with effervescence and also soluble in cyanide of potassium solutions ; it is employed in the preparation of brass baths ; it is best used in plastic form.

Nickel Carbonate.—A pale blue-green substance, insoluble in water and soluble with effervescence in acids; it is principally employed in nickel baths to neutralize same which has become acid and increases the metallic strength at the same time. By the addition of ammonia, a greenish precipitate is formed, which, with an excess of ammonia, is redissolved, forming a beautiful blue color ; it is best used in plastic form.

Ammonium Sulphate.—This is a colorless, neutral salt, does not effloresce in the air ; readily soluble in water ; it is used principally as a conducting salt for nickel and zinc solutions.

Iron Sulphate or Copperas.—Blue green transparent crystals ; readily dissolved in hot water ; oxydizes in the air ; employed principally for the preparation of iron baths and for reducing gold from its solution.

Iron Ammonium Sulphate.—Used for the same purpose as copperas.

Copper Sulphate or Blue Vitriol.—Beautiful blue crystals, soluble in cold water ; more readily soluble in hot water ; used principally in the preparation of copper and brass baths and electrotyper's copper solution.

Zinc Sulphate. (White Vitriol).—Small colorless crystals readily oxydized in the air ; are soluble in both cold and hot water ; used principally in the preparation of brass and zinc baths.

Nickel Sulphate.—Beautiful dark-green crystals ; soluble in water, forming a green solution ; used principally in the preparation of nickel baths.

Nickel Ammonia Sulphate.---Green crystals ; dissolving slightly in cold water and readily in hot water. Is the principal salt of nickel employed in nickel plating.

Sodium Bisulphite.---Small crystals used principally in the preparation of copper and brass baths.

Sodium Hyposulphite.---Transparent white crystals used principally in brass and gold baths.

Mercuric Nitrate.—Small colorless crystals, transparent ; it is employed for amalgamating the zincs in electric batteries.

Silver Nitrate Crystals.—Is thin transparent crystals; dissolves readily in water ; used principally for making silver solutions.

Pyrophosphate of Soda.—White crystals which do not effloresce ; not readily soluble in cold water; soluble in hot water ; it is used in the preparation of gold and tin baths.

Potassium Bitartrate. (Cream of tartar).—Small transparent crystals, soluble in water ; employed in silvering paste and also in tin baths.

Copper Acetate. (Verdigris).—Green crystals, usually sold commercially in the form of pale green powder ; dissolve with difficulty in water ; readily soluble in ammonia, forming a beautiful blue liquid ; also soluble in cyanide of potassium and alkaline sulphites ; it is used in the preparation of copper and brass baths and for coloring, gilding, etc.

Lead Acetate. (Sugar of lead).—Colorless crystals; poisonous ; readily soluble in water ; employed in the preparation of lead baths and for coloring copper and brass.

Cleaning Compound, 381.—This is a light yellowish hard mass, partly soluble in cold water, soluble in hot water, and is used for cleaning rouge, composition, etc., from iron and steel articles and large brass work after plating and buffing.   It is also used before plating.

Cleaning Compound, 681.—This is a dark brown soft mass, partly soluble in cold water, soluble in hot water, having the odor of ammonia.   It is used for the same purpose as the 381 Cleaning Compound, except that it is used on small brass work, Britannia metal, silver, gold, nickel-plated articles, etc.

Salicornia Lye.—This is a white granular powder ; absorbs moisture from the air and is used for cleaning grease and dirt from metals before plating, taking the place of potash or soda.

CHAPTER XXIII.

ARTICLES USED IN POLISHING ROOM.

Tripoli Composition.—This is in brick form of a light yellowish color. It is used principally for "cutting down" or polishing all metals except iron and steel.

Crocus Composition.—This is both in brick and padded form, of a dark chocolate brown color It is used principally for "cutting down" or polishing all metals and sometimes for "coloring" or buffing iron, steel and nickel plated iron or steel where a very high finish is not desired.

Emery Cake.—This is in brick form, of a black or dark grey color, and is made in different grades of fineness. It is used principally for "roughing up" or polishing articles of iron or steel and very rough brass.

Emery Paste.—This is a black or dark grey mass put up in cartridge form and is used for the same purpose as emery cake.

Patent Emery Compound.—This is in brick form, of a black or dark grey color, with a yellow coating. It is principally used for making a grease wheel instead of the old method. This is done by simply applying the stick to the wheel, either felt or leather, while it is revolving on the lathe, and after a sufficient quantity has adhered, smooth same down with a flat stone. It is also used on canvas, sheepskin or muslin buffs for "cutting down" or polishing stove and other cast iron and steel work, also sheet brass and tubes.

Sand Buffing Composition.—This is in brick form,

of a light grey color. It is used principally on tampico wheel brushes for buffing sheet brass.

Patent Black Composition.—This is in brick form, of a jet black color. It is principally used for polishing horn and hard rubber, but is excellent for quick cutting down brass.

Snowflake Polish.—This is in brick form, of a whitish color. It is used for "coloring" or buffing nickel plated work, also brass, copper and aluminum.

Patent White Polish.—This is in brick form, and is of a pure white color with a yellowish coating. It is used principally for buffing nickel plated work, to which it imparts a superior lustre. It is also excellent for coloring brass, copper, bronze, etc.

Rouge.—This is in stick and powdered form, of a bright red color. It is used for "coloring" or buffing all metals. There are various grades of this article, the grade to be used depending upon the metal which it is intended to buff.

"Oxytin" or Putty Powder.—This is a light yellow or white powder. It is used principally for polishing marble, granite, glass, onyx, etc.

Pumice.—This is in irregular lumps of various sizes and also in powdered form of different grades of fineness. It is used for scouring iron and steel, for sand buffing and also quite extensively for grinding glass.

Emery.—This is a black or dark grey powder of various degrees of fineness. It is principally used on leather wheels of different kinds, also on strapping belts and canvas wheels for grinding iron, steel and brass, also glass.

Emery Glue.—This is in flake or powdered form, and is used for coating wheels of various kinds in order to hold the emery to them.

Vienna Lime.—This is in both lump and powdered form. It is used principally for dry buffing or "wiping off."

Buffs. (Mops).—These are formed of a number of layers and are made of various kinds of muslin, etc., and are used on lathes for polishing and buffing all metals, the material depending upon the class of work ; bleached muslin, printers' ink, patent white and patent piece sewed buffs being generally used for "cutting down" or polishing and unbleached muslin and canton flannel buffs for "coloring" or buffing.

Polishing Wheels.—These are leather covered wood wheels, solid leather wheels of walrus, bullneck, buff leather, etc., canvas, sheepskin and felt. For grinding and polishing, the leather wheels are "set up" with emery and glue, the canvas and sheepskin with patent emery compound, and the felt with emery and glue or patent emery compound, but in the case of buffing, for which felt is often used, with crocus composition, patent white polish or rouge.

Solid Emery Wheels.—These are of various grades of fineness, and are used solely for grinding.

Polishing or Strapping Belts.—These are of various kinds, principally of rubber and canvas, or canvas alone, sewed. They are used on belt strapping machines set up with emery and glue for polishing parts of articles which it is impossible to do on wheels.

Scouring or Platers' Brushes.—These are made of tampico and bristles, and are from one to six row. They are used for cleaning and scouring the work before and after plating.

Potash Brushes.—These are made of cotton and are used for cleaning work where salicornia lye or potash is used.

Wheel Brushes.—These are circular in form and are made of tampico and bristles. They are used principally with emery and oil or patent emery compound, for polishing sheet brass, etc.

Scratch Brushes.—These are circular in form and are made of brass, steel, German silver and copper wire of different guages. They are used for various purposes, namely : cleaning castings, smoothing, polishing and matting all metals, the kind and guage of wire used depending upon the class of work.

CHAPTER XXIV.
USEFUL INFORMATION.

Transmission of Power. —In all mechanical processes it is very important that the means for the transmission of power should be carefully considered. In this regard there are several points to be observed.

Hangers should be in perfect alignment, and not too far apart ; shafting should be straight and not too small ; and pulleys should be as light as possible, consistent with strength, and well balanced.

Countershafts should not be run at high speed. This can be avoided by making the driving pulley as large as possible. In this way a greater belt velocity can be obtained on the driving pulley without increasing its revolutions.

Wood pulleys in most cases are preferable to iron ones, as they weigh much less and will transmit more power, the friction on them being greater. The face of pulleys should be crowned, as in this way they will overcome in a measure the defects of non-alignment.

Belts should be run with their hair side against the pulleys, as that side will give greater friction. By using a first-class belt dressing the adhesion is increased and the tension of the belt may in a degree be reduced, thereby lessening the friction on bearings and saving power. Vertical belts should be avoided, as in this position they must be stretched tight on the pulleys to gain any adhesion.

Two pulleys of greatly different diameters should not be belted too near to each other, as the angle or arc of contact between belt and pulley is what determines the friction or driving capacity of a belt. The angle of contact on the smaller one being comparitively small, would render it liable to slip.

HOW TO CALCULATE SPEED AND DIAMETERS OF PULLEYS.

Let A represent diameter of driving pulley.

Let B represent revolutions per minute of driving pulley.

Let C represent diameter of driven pulley.

Let D represent revolutions per minute of driven pulley.

To find D multiply A by B and divide by C.

To find C multiply A by B and divide by D.

To find B multiply D by C and divide by A.

To find A multiply D by C and divide by B.

DIRECTIONS FOR CALCULATING THE WIDTH OF BELTS REQUIRED FOR TRANSMITTING DIFFERENT NUMBERS OF HORSE-POWER.

Multiply 33,000 by the numbers of horse power to be transmitted, divide the amount by the number of feet the belt is to run per minute ; divide the quotient by the number of feet or parts of a foot in length of belt contact with smaller drum or pulley ; divide the last quotient by six, and the result is the required width of a leather belt in inches.

Explanations.—The figure 33,000 represents the number of pounds a horse is reckoned to be able to raise one foot high in a minute. To obtain the number of feet a belt runs in a minute find the number of revolutions per minute of the driving shaft and multiply by the circumference of the drum, which is always 3.1416 its diameter. The final division by six is because half a pound raised one foot high per minute is allowed to each square inch of belting in contact with the pulley ; a pound must, therefore, be allowed to two square inches, or six pounds to a strip one foot long and one inch wide.

Example.---Required the width of a single belt, the velocity of which is to be 1,500 feet per minute ; it has to transmit 10 horse-power, the diameter of the smaller drum being four feet with five feet of its circumference in contact with the belt.

$$33,000 \times 10 = 330,000 \div 1,500 = 220 \div 5 = 44 - 6 = 7\tfrac{1}{2}$$

inches, the required width of belt.

DIRECTIONS FOR CALCULATING THE NUMBER OF HORSE=POWER WHICH A BELT WILL TRANSMIT.

Divide the number of square inches of belt in contact with the pulley by two ; multiply this quotient by the velocity of the belt in feet per minute ; again we divide the total by 33,000 and the quotient is the number of horse-power.

Explanations.—The early division by two is to obtain the number of pounds raised one foot high per minute, half a pound being allowed to each square inch of belting in contact with the pulley.

Example.---A six-inch single belt is being moved with a velocity of 1,200 feet per minute, with four feet of its length in contact with a three foot drum.   Required the horse-power :

6×48=288÷2=144×1,200=172,800÷33,000=say 5¼ horse-power.

It is safe to reckon that a double belt will do half as much work again as a single one.

Hints to Users of Belts.—1.   Horizontal, inclined and long belts give a much better effect than vertical and short belts.

2.   Short belts require to be tighter than long ones. A long belt working horizontally increases the grip by its own weight.

3.   If there is too great a distance between the pulleys, the weight of the belt will produce a heavy sag, drawing so hard on the shaft as to cause great friction at the bearings, while at the same time the belt will have an unsteady motion, injurious to itself and to the machinery.

CONTENTS OF VESSELS.

To find the number gallons a tank or other vessel will hold, divide the number of cubic inches it contains by 231.

If rectangular, multiply together the length, breadth and depth.

If cylindrical, multiply the square of the diameter by 0.7854, and the product by the depth.

If conical, add together squares of diameters of top and bottom, and the product of the two diameters. Multiply their sum by 0.7854, and the resulting product by the depth.   Divide the product by 3.

If hemispherical, to three times the square of the radius at top add the square of the depth. Multiply this sum by the depth and the product by 0.5236.

AVOIRDUPOIS WEIGHT.

	=Ounces.	= Drams.	= Grains.	= Grams.
1 Pound.........	16	256	7,000	453.25
1 Ounce....	1	16	437.5	28.33
1 Dram..........	0.062	1	27.34	1.77

TROY WEIGHT.

	= Ounces.	= Dwt.	= Grains.	= Grams.
1 Pound.........	12	240	5,760	372.96
1 Ounce.........	1	20	480	31.08
1 Pennyweight...	0.05	1	24	1.55

IMPERIAL FLUID MEASURE.

	= Quart.	= Pints.	= Fluid Ounces.	= Fluid Drams.	= Minims.	= Weight in Grains.	= Cubic Inches.	= Liters.	= Cubic Centimeters.
1 Gallon......	4	8	160	1280	76,800	70.000	277.276	4.541	4,541
1 Quart.... ...	1	2	40	320	19,200	17,500	69.319	1.135	1,135.2
1 Pint......	0.5	1	20	160	9,600	8,750	34.659	0.567	576.6
1 Fluid Ounce...	0.025	0.05	1	8	480	437.5	1.733	0.0284	283.8
1 Fluid Dram....	0.0031	0.0062	0.125	1	60	54.7	0.217	0.0035	35.5
1 Minim......	0.00005	0.0001	0.0021	0.0167	1	0.91	0.0036	0.00006	0.59

NUMERICAL RELATIONS OF THERMOMETRIC SCALES.

9 Fahrenheit degrees equal 5 Centigrade degrees, or 4 Reaumur dagrees.

To convert—

Fahr. to Cent.	. .subtract	... 32	multiply by....5	and divide by	9
" " Reaumur....	"	 32	" " 4	" " "	9
Cent. " Fahr.	...multiply by	... 9	divide by......5	and add......	32
" " Reaumur ...	"	" ... 4	and divide by..5		
Reaumur to Fahr....	"	" 9	divide by......4	and add.......	32
" " Cent....	"	" ... 5	and divide by..4		

Example to convert 212 Fahr. to Centigrade....... .....

$$
\begin{array}{r}
212 \\
32 \\
\hline
180 \\
5 \\
\hline
9)900 \\
\hline
100 \text{ Cent.}
\end{array}
$$

- - - -- -----------

TABLE OF USEFUL NUMERICAL DATA.

1 millimeter equals.................. .03937 inches.

1 centimeter "   .... .39370 "

1 decimeter "   .... 3.93700 "

1 meter "   ....39.37000 "

1 cubic centimeter of } ....1 Gram.
water equals..... }

1 liter "   .... 1000. "

1 "   "   ....{ .... 35.275 { ounces by measure.

1 gallon (or 160 fluid } ... . 4.536 liters.
ounces) equals..... }

1 gallon "   .. ..277.276 cubic inches.

1 pint (or 20 fluid } .... 34.659 "   "
ounces) equals .. }

1 fluid ounce equals .... 1.733 "   "

1 liter "   .... 61.024 "   "

1 avoirdupois } .... 7000. grains.
pound equals... }

1 troy pound equals.................5760,   grains.

1 avoirdupois ounce equals.............. 437.5   "

1 troy ounce equals................. 480.   "

1 avoirdupois drm. equals..................27.34   "

1 troy pennyweight equals..................24.   "

1 gram equals..................... 15.43   "

1 kilogram " ....15432.   "

1 liter of water equals...............15432.   "

1 cubic inch of water equals.............. 252.5   "

1 cubic centimeter of water equals................ 1.   gram.

1 kilogram equals................. .....35.274 avoirdupois ozs.

TABLE OF ELECTRIC CONDUCTING POWERS
OF METALS.
(Mathieson.)

	Conducting Powers.		Conducting Powers.
Silver.......... ...100.		Tin............... 12.4
Copper........... 99.9		Thallium.......... 9.2
Gold............ 77.9		Lead............. 8.3
Zinc .... 29.		Arsenic........... 4.8
Cadmium.......... 23.7		Antimony....... .. 4.6
Platinum..... .... 18.		Mercury.......... 1.6
Cobalt 17.2		Bismuth.......... 1.2
Iron............ 16.8		Graphite.......... .069
Nickel............ 13.1		Gas Coke......... .038

ANTIDOTES FOR POISONS USED IN THE PLATING ROOM.

Nitric, Hydrochloric or Sulphuric Acids.—Administer abundance of tepid water to act as an emetic, or swallow milk, the whites of eggs, some calcined magnesia, or a mixture of chalk and water. If those acids, in a concentrated state, have been spilled on the skin, apply a mixture of whiting and olive oil. If the quantity is very small, simple swilling with plenty of cold water will suffice. A useful mixture, in cases of burning with strong sulphuric acid, is formed with one ounce of quicklime slaked with a quarter of an ounce of water, then adding it to a quart of water. After standing some time, pour off the clear liquid and mix it with olive oil to form a thin paste.

Potassium Cyanide, Hydrocyanic Acid, etc.—If cyanides, such as a drop of an ordinary plating solution, has been accidently swallowed, water, as cold as possible, should be run on the head and spine of the sufferer, and a dilute solution of iron acetate, citrate, or tartrate administered. If hydrocyanic acid vapors have been inhaled, cold water should be applied as above, and the patient be caused to inhale atmospheric air containing a little chlorine gas. It is a dangerous practice to dip the arms into a plating solution to recover any work that has fallen off the wires, because the skin often absorbs cyanide liquids, causing painful sores. In such a case, wash well with water, and apply the olive oil and lime water mixture.

Alkalies.—These bodies are the opposite of acids in character, so that acids may be used as antidotes. It is preferable to employ weak acids, such as vinegar or lemonade ; but if these are not at hand, then use exceedingly dilute sulphuric acid or even nitric acid diluted, so that it just possesses a decidedly sour taste. After about ten minutes take a few teaspoonfuls of olive oil.

Mercury Salts.—The white of an egg is the best antidote in this case. Sulphur and sulphuretted hydrogen are also serviceable for the purpose.

Copper Salts.—The stomach should be quickly emptied by means of an emetic, or in want of this, the patient should thrust his finger to the back of his throat so as to tickle the uvula, and thus induce vomiting. After vomiting, drink milk, white of an egg, or gum water.

Lead Salts.—Proceed as in case of copper salts. Lemonade, soda water and sodium carbonate are also serviceable.

Acid Vapors.—Admit immediately an abundance of fresh air, and inhale the vapors of ammonia, or a few drops of ammonia may be put into a glass of water and the solution drunk. Take plenty of hot drinks and excite warmth by friction. Employ hot foot-baths to remove the blood from the lungs. Keep the throat moist by sipping milk.

Removal of Stains, etc.—To remove stains of copper sulphate, or salts of mercury, gold, silver, etc., from the hands, wash them with a very dilute solution of ammonia, and then with plenty of water ; if the stains are old ones they should be rubbed with the strongest acetic acid, and then treated as above.

Grease, oil, tar, etc., may be removed from the hands or clothes by rubbing with a rag saturated with benzine, turpentine, or carbon bi-sulphide.

INDEX.

107

PAGE.

109

113

114

www.ingramcontent.com/pod-product-compliance
Lightning Source LLC
Chambersburg PA
CBHW032111010726
47493CB00008B/2539